A PUZZLE IN PEARLS

A Puzzle in Pearls

A Patrick Dawlish Mystery

John Creasey *writing as* Gordon Ashe

OPEN ROAD

INTEGRATED MEDIA
NEW YORK

Copyright © 1949 by John Creasey

ISBN: 978-1-5040-9818-2

This edition published in 2025 by Open Road Integrated Media, Inc.
180 Maiden Lane
New York, NY 10038
www.openroadmedia.com

A PUZZLE IN PEARLS

CHAPTER 1

THE HUNTER

'This,' said Roger Macclesfield firmly, 'is ridiculous. Chasing after a girl I don't know, like a hot-blooded Lothario. It must stop.'

The girl who occupied so much of his thoughts was hidden by a large, uneven rock, a romantic relic mentioned in Brittling guide books. Then she appeared again on the winding path, a few yards from the cliff's edge; and Roger's heart turned over in an absurd, unreasoning way.

He ran his hand through his thick, brown hair and took a step forward.

'No!' he cried aloud, and stopped again.

It was September, and the holiday-makers were thinning out, nevertheless he was sure he would have noticed her in a thousand. He had seen her only three times, the last being an enticing glimpse as she walked from *The Bay Hotel*, the most luxurious in Brittling, and entered a sleek and powerful limousine. In the half-light her eyes had sparkled up at her handsome escort. Then she had gone laughingly off with her party of young people whom Roger had envied with unreasoning fervour.

A car came bumping over the grass behind him as he walked towards the rock in the wake of the unknown girl.

She would soon be out of sight again, behind a clump of wind-driven trees which leaned drunkenly away from the sea.

But for his preoccupation he would have known that the people in the car were taking some interest in him. There were three men. Their car had stopped, and now they were standing by the dark saloon, watching him.

The girl disappeared.

Roger flung himself moodily down on the grass, and fumbled in his pockets for pipe and pouch.

This was the last time he would make a fool of himself over that girl or any other. It might have been different if he, himself, were staying at the *Bay Hotel*, or stood the slightest chance of meeting her in any orthodox fashion.

A motor-boat came chugging towards the cliffs. He noticed it idly. The cliff-edge was broken here, and there was a path down to a half-hidden cove. It was a small boat, painted blue-grey, with two men in it. It disappeared from view, cut off by the cliff.

He looked towards the right.

The girl had appeared again, but was too far off for him to catch up with her, even if he allowed his resolve to weaken.

A man came round the rock and appeared in front of him. Roger first saw dusty black shoes and the ends of a pair of well-pressed trousers.

The stranger said tentatively: 'I wonder if I could trouble you for a match?'

'No trouble,' muttered Roger.

He took out a box of matches and held them up. The hand which took them was lean and brown and scarred across the back. That much Roger noticed particularly, and the fact that the man was bearded.

'Thanks,' said the other. 'Nice morning.'

'Love—' began Roger.

Pain streaked across the back of his neck suddenly, agonisingly. His head seemed to split in two. Where there had been brightness there was a red mist, growing rapidly darker. Then blackness.

The pain was still there, but it wasn't dark. Much too bright, in fact; dazzlingly, hurtfully bright. Roger opened his eyes, then closed them abruptly. Unbearable. And how his head ached! Presently his lashes flickered, cautiously, experimentally. Earth. So he was on the side of the cliff, not at the top. When he looked up he could see the spiky, long grass sticking out at the edge.

Tenderly he felt the back of his head; he winced. He drew his hand away, half-expecting to see blood, but his fingers were quite dry.

He remembered the bearded man and the blow; a bearded man—a car—a motor-boat—the girl. The bearded man had distracted his attention and one of the others from the car had hit him. Three men and a powerful car and a blue-grey motor-boat, the girl, and his own folly—but for that he wouldn't be here now. So in a way it was his own fault. Well, hardly. One didn't expect to be set upon by a gang of ruffians when one followed a charming girl at a distance along the edge of a cliff.

Had he been *thrown* down here?

The thought sobered him. He sat up and looked about him. He was fifty yards down, and a hundred yards or more from the sea. If he had been tossed over, then it was sheer luck that he was alive. Callous devils! But wait a minute, they might have carried him here. The path wasn't far away, and he could see footprints in the sandy track. Possibly they had chosen this spot so that he wouldn't be seen from the top.

He moved to one side cautiously.

It was then that he saw the pearls.

They lay just beyond his reach, between him and the path. He eased himself nearer and picked them up. He knew nothing about pearls. These *looked* real enough, but he couldn't tell the difference between real and cultured. He held them up and stared at them. They couldn't be real, they were too big, too casually lost. He slipped them into his pocket, his whole attention bent now on how to get back to the path. One dizzy moment and he would fall, and probably break his neck.

He peered up at the cliff-top.

He must shout of course, it was the only thing to do; someone would pass along the top of the cliff before long, and come to the rescue. At least no bones were broken; he could move fairly freely. Better wait for a while.

He heard something; a quiet sound, as of sand and soil falling. He looked towards the path and saw a small stone roll a little way and then come to a stop. Here was the help he needed, thank heavens—and he could get it without making a fuss. As he stared towards the path a foot came in sight, and a trim, bare, tanned ankle, then a companion foot—and the girl.

CHAPTER 2

THE HUNTED

The girl was bending towards him.

'Do you want to get up or down the cliff?' she asked. 'I'd advise down, the slope isn't so steep.'

Her eyes matched her hair: tawny, with golden flecks, the lashes unusually long and curved.

He had heard her speak before but had not realised how husky and unusually deep her voice was. He didn't speak; he couldn't.

'Wouldn't you like a cigarette?' she asked.

The sun beat on his head and face, making his head throb; there were strange noises in his ears, and he felt not just foolish but completely inane. He had the wit to understand that she would probably put his inanity down to his 'fall', which gave him some solace.

She took a small cigarette case, a pretty gilt-and-enamel thing, and a lighter, from a pocket, lit a cigarette and then took it from her lips and put it to his. He muttered his thanks, and she smiled and looked out to sea, so that her profile was towards him. The thing he liked best was the tilt of her head and the way her pointed chin was raised. He was vaguely aware of some perfume, of the innumerable pleats in the full skirt of her dress, open like a fan now, and the way she hugged her knees.

She turned and looked at him.

'I wish I could offer you a drink,' she said, 'but the nearest place is the beach café, and that's nearly three miles away. If you like, I'll go and get you one.'

'I—I shouldn't dream of letting you go so far,' said Roger, finding his voice. 'I'll be all right in a few minutes. In fact I'm all right now.' He put a hand to the ground.

'Better finish the cigarette before you get up,' the girl advised.

She looked away quickly, and he began to wonder what to tell her. The truth? It wouldn't be easy to convince anyone that his story was true. It would be much better to say he'd slipped; if he started to tell the truth she would think he was romancing, and talking for effect.

The cigarette was nearly finished when she turned to look at him again.

'Did the man have a beard?' she asked.

The question so startled Roger that he moved, and the loose earth on which he was sitting slipped from under him. She shot out a hand to steady him, and caught his wrist in cool, firm fingers.

'B-beard?' he echoed weakly.

'You see, I saw everything, or nearly everything,' she told him calmly. 'I was sitting on the trunk of a tree, and wondering why that car had come across the grass. And then I saw the men approach you, and—well, you know the rest of it,' she finished. 'But I wasn't sure about the beard.'

'Oh, yes, he had a beard,' said Roger slowly. 'Did you say you saw *everything*?'

'I'd forgotten, you don't know what happened after they hit you,' the girl said calmly. 'They carried you as far as this, and then hurried down to the cove, got into the motor-boat, and went off. That is, two of them did. The third man returned to the top of the cliff, and drove off in the car. Everything was over in less than ten minutes, long before I could get here.'

'Oh,' said Roger.

He was relieved that she knew the truth and there was no need to lie to her.

He tossed the cigarette away.

'It was extraordinary bad luck that you happened to stop just where they wanted to get down to the boat,' she remarked before he could speak.

'And extraordinary good luck that the brutes didn't throw me into the sea,' said Roger drily. He struggled up. 'I think I could manage to get down now.'

She sprang to her feet.

'Splendid. Let me help.' She stretched out her hands; he took them, and she pulled steadily. In a moment he was standing upright—and the next he lurched forward and flung his arms around her, and to save them both from falling she hugged him. They swayed on the precarious perch, like two lovers in a moment of ecstasy. He saw the gay laughter in her eyes, as she gently disengaged herself.

'Sorry about that,' he said heavily.

'We ought to have expected it,' said the girl. 'Just edge this way a little, and then we'll manage it all right.'

Going down was at once a dream and a nightmare. Every now and again he slipped, and would have fallen but for her help. Exhausted, his forehead dripping with sweat, he finally made it.

'Shall we try to walk?' she asked. 'It's not so difficult on the wet sand, and the tide's going out, so we'll be able to walk along to the beach café without any trouble.'

They started off easily enough, though more often than he cared about he was forced to rest. At the fourth stop he groped in his pocket, and scowled. He tried in his other pocket. It must be at the top of the cliff.

'What have you lost?' she asked.

'Pipe,' said Roger.

'I expect it'll still be on the top of the cliff,' said the girl. 'We'll go after it.'

'So you come from a pipe-loving family,' remarked Roger.

Her eyes shone with merriment.

'My father and two brothers hate cigarettes almost as much as they hate cocktails.'

'Are they here in Brittling?' he asked in surprise.

'They were due at ten o'clock, and it's past that now—in fact,' the girl said, glancing at a small, gold watch on her wrist, 'it's nearly eleven. Just for the weekend. They'll be waiting at the hotel, and of course they'll refuse to believe a word I tell them about the attack.'

Roger's fingers closed over the forgotten string of pearls and he drew them out of his pocket wonderingly. He held them up to the light, and saw that their lustre was quite remarkable—they looked much more beautiful now than when he had first examined them. The girl looked at them in astonishment.

'Nice, aren't they?' he observed.

'Nice!'

'Well, pretty,' said Roger, 'or whatever the proper word is. I've just remembered that I found them on the path.'

She took them from him, examining them closely, her expression one of intensity and interest. It was a long time before she lowered the pearls and looked at him.

'So, you've found a fortune,' she remarked.

'Fortune?' he answered in surprise. 'But they can't be real!'

'They most certainly are,' said the girl, slowly. 'I think I am beginning to see what it was all about.'

CHAPTER 3

THE BROTHERS

She thought that he had been attacked by thieves who were taking their loot out of the country by the motor-boat; and certainly that seemed feasible. They did not talk much about it, but he was very conscious of the pearls in his pocket as they started off again. The tide was now far out, and they met little parties of adults and children playing on the hard, damp sand.

It was nearly twelve o'clock before they reached the beach café. They had coffee and biscuits at a verandah table, saying very little; the girl seemed to take him for granted, and her quietness was companionable.

Not far from the café was a cliff lift, and soon they were at the top of the cliff, mingling with crowds which became more dense the nearer they drew to the centre of Brittling. The *Bay Hotel* was just beyond the pier, and they still had about a mile to go when Roger first noticed the two men.

They were walking on the other side of the road which flanked the promenade. Dressed in flannels and sports jackets, they were apparently uninterested in anything or anybody, but now and again they looked across the road towards him and the girl. One of them was bearded, and reminded Roger vividly of the man who had asked him for a match.

He quickened his pace.

He did not think the girl had noticed the men, and he did not want to alarm her. Surely no violence could happen here! But— the men who had attacked him might realise that he had found the pearls, and if the girl was right and the pearls were real, then violent efforts might be made to get them back. Roger's heart beat fast.

He glanced round—and saw that the men had separated. The beardless one had just passed them. The other was falling in behind, as if to hem them in.

Then the man who had forged ahead swung round and faced them. Roger sent a frantic glance over his shoulder and saw the bearded man only a few yards away. *Was* it his assailant?

'Oh!' exclaimed the girl.

The exclamation might have sprung from alarm or any other emotion. In a few long strides the beardless man was within arm's length.

'Peter!' exclaimed the girl.

'"Peter" it is, and who, may I or may I not ask, is your latest young man?'

'Precisely,' said a remarkably deep voice behind them. 'And I second that.'

'Adam!' cried the girl, spinning round, her face alive with pleasure.

'We are waiting to be introduced,' Peter announced.

He ranged himself on Roger's left and the bearded brother— for who else could these be?—ranged himself on the girl's right. Side by side, they stretched halfway across the prom-enade.

All four were now walking in step.

'He's probably decided that she's not nice to know,' said Adam. 'If the bump on the back of his head is anything to go by, she's been at her tantrums again. Dangerous woman, my sister,' he added.

'Be warned, and have nothing to do with her,' advised Peter.

'I entirely endorse that,' remarked his brother. 'And may I remind you, Angela my pet, that we are still waiting to be introduced.'

'And so am I,' said Angela, laughing.

A startled look appeared in Peter's eyes; a blank one in Adam's.

'Old chap, don't think I'm curious, or anything like that, but—you aren't one of those unfortunates who thinks silence is golden, are you?'

Roger opened his mouth.

'I think he's shown good sense,' said Angela firmly. 'Anyone meeting you two for the first time ought to say nothing—or at least count ten before he says what he thinks of you. You've guessed they are my brothers, haven't you?' she asked Roger. 'I love them so much when they're away, but when they're with me I begin to hate the sight and sound of them.'

'How she babbles!' said Peter.

'And that reminds me,' said Adam, pausing, 'there is a hostelry across the road where I'm told the beer's not bad.'

'No, he mustn't drink yet,' said Angela hastily.

'Ignore the wench,' said Peter. 'I've a suspicion that she's a secret teetotaller, she always hates us to go into pubs and would forbid us the bar if she could.'

'That's a whopper,' said Angela, 'but his head—'

'Ah, yes, his head,' said Adam. 'How did you do it? Push him over the cliff and then pretend to rescue him?'

'*What?*' ejaculated Roger.

'He has spoken!' boomed Adam. 'There's no oral impedi-ment. Beer?'

'Look here—' began Angela.

'Silence,' ordered Adam. 'The oracle will speak.'

Roger burst into laughter which brought a responding gleam to the brother's eyes. Without a word they all trooped into the *Mary Anne*. It was pleasantly cool in the saloon bar, and they were lucky enough to get a corner table.

The drinks having arrived, Roger put his tankard down and said quietly:

'Having met you all, it's only fair you should meet me. Name, Roger Macclesfield. Age, twenty-nine. Recreations, being bumped over the head and purloining pearls.'

'How do you do,' said the brothers simultaneously.

'So nice to meet you,' said Angela. 'Our other name is Boon.'

'But how *did* you meet?' asked Peter.

Angela began to tell them . . .

During the telling a change came over the two young men. They took her seriously. When at last Angela reached the subject of the pearls she stretched out her hand demandingly.

Roger dropped them into her palm. Her brothers glanced at them, but did not speak until she had finished. She put the pearls on the tile-topped table, and after a pause, Adam said:

'Oh, they're real.'

'Worth a fabulous fortune,' remarked Peter casually.

'Your safest course is certainly the police, although—'

'The police,' said Angela firmly.

'The honoured parent first,' said Peter, finishing his beer. 'Coming?'

They trooped out.

After the dimness of the bar the sun seemed even hotter.

Traffic was thick, and the crowds at the pier-head so dense that people spilled into the roadway.

It was too crowded to walk abreast now, so the brothers let Angela and Roger walk ahead, and followed a few yards behind. They turned off the main road along a narrow street at the foot of a steep hill which led to the *Bay Hotel*.

A tall man, strolling from the gateway, caught sight of them and quickened his pace. Angela waved. Roger caught a glimpse of the man's handsome face, his grey hair swept back from his forehead, and his bright, shrewd eyes.

'Meet a piece of adventure off the cliff,' sang out Adam. 'Roger Macclesfield, our father, Colonel Martin Boon.'

Roger said: 'How are you, sir?'

'Hallo,' said Boon. 'I hope my children haven't been too over-powering. You're having lunch with us, I hope.'

'Of course he is,' said Angela. 'I'll tell you all about it as we walk up,' she added, taking her father's arm.

No one else was in the narrow street which was a *cul de sac* serving the *Bay Hotel* and several smaller hotels. In the grounds, just visible beyond a high, white wall, palm trees stirred in the gentle wind, and a great oak spread wide branches.

A car turned into the *cul de sac* and came humming towards them but Roger, with a brother on either side, hardly noticed it. He watched Angela and her father, as they disappeared into the gateway of the hotel. At the same moment the car drew up.

The driver leaned out.

'Excuse me, sir, but is this the way to *Bay Hotel*?'

'The drive's on the other—' began Peter helpfully, and broke off. A gun was pointing straight at him.

The rear door of the car shot open, and two men climbed out, ranging themselves quickly on either side of the Boons and Roger.

'We don't want any trouble,' said the driver, 'but you'll get it all right if you ask for it. We want the pearls.'

As he spoke one of the men grabbed Roger's arm, twisted it behind him, and pushed him towards the car.

CHAPTER 4

THE THIEVES

The gun covered the brothers steadily, and they stood still. Roger was pushed forward by the two men behind him. The low roof of the car loomed up, and he ducked too late, cracking his head against the top of the door. The blow almost knocked him out, and he sagged back.

'Get in!' rasped a voice in his ear.

Adam Boon, nearest the driver, raised a leg and kicked the door to, shutting the driver in and cutting the gun off for an all-important second. Then he drove his first through the open window into the driver's face.

Peter back-heeled as his brother moved, and hacked one of the other two on the shin. A grunt of pain told him how well he had aimed.

The cry also told Roger's captor that the Boons were making a fight. He relaxed his grip, flinging Roger to the ground.

Behind him Peter was grappling with one of the assailants, but the third man jumped to the rescue and punched Peter on the side of the jaw. The engine roared as the driver trod on the accelerator.

The car swept round the end of the *cul-de-sac*, making for the bottom of the hill.

Recalled by the uproar, Angela and her father appeared in the gateway. Angela broke into a run, while Adam raised his voice and called:

'Registration—2AK21. Got it? 2AK21!'

'Yes,' said Colonel Boon, and disappeared again.

The car had already turned the corner and was out of sight. Neither of the Boon brothers wasted time running after it. They helped Roger to his feet and all three walked, a little painfully, towards the gateway. Two or three people were looking over the wall, and a little man hurried across the road to them. Peter stayed to answer his questions, while Roger, angry with himself because he felt so helpless, allowed himself to be led towards the gate and then up a flight of steep steps until he was on the hotel level.

A majestic-looking woman came up to them.

'Did I hear you call *police*?'

'Fool with a car,' said Adam brusquely. 'Knocked my friend down—no great harm done.'

'How disgraceful!'

'Disgraceful's the word,' agreed Adam.

The hall was cool.

The lift was waiting.

Presently Roger found himself in a large, luxurious room of soft creams and greens. He sank into an easy chair, praying for the Boon faces to stop whirling round him, and settle solidly to anchor on their shoulders again.

Although he certainly did not feel at his best, Roger was soon very much better. The Boons proved themselves to be a capable family. First aid had been administered with speed and competence, and now, in a borrowed jacket of Adam's, he sat in an armchair sipping a cup of hot coffee which one of them had conjured from a reluctant floor-waiter.

Not one of the four Boons appeared to be flustered or indignant. Indeed, they accepted the situation with unnerving calmness.

A clock outside struck one.

'What time are they bringing lunch?' asked Adam.

'Half past one,' said Colonel Boon. 'I thought that would give us time to talk to the police and then eat in comfort. The police should be here by now,' he added. 'You'll be glad to be rid of those pearls, Macclesfield, won't you?'

'I shall,' said Roger feelingly. He dropped his hand to his pocket and then remembered that he was wearing a borrowed coat.

'Exhibit for the police,' said Adam cheerfully, 'your coat's still in the bathroom.'

To Roger, a man of few friends and fewer relations, the way this family accepted him was heartening. The Boons had a dream-quality; a family which was really closely held by ties of friendship, each part of the whole and yet so markedly individual. The one characteristic which appeared common to them all was this calmness in an unusual situation.

Roger thought fleetingly of his assailants and the daring of their attack. That they were desperately anxious to get the pearls went without saying. So, therefore, did the value of the jewels.

Footsteps sounded in the passage.

'Ready to face 'em?' asked Adam.

At that moment Roger saw something in the Colonel's eyes which hadn't been there before. It was wariness; he felt that Boon was steeling himself for this interview. Absurd? The impression passed swiftly, and yet Roger could not forget it. He looked at the others. Was it imagination, or was there a pause, almost of indecision, before a heavy knock came at the door?

Angela glanced towards it. Roger fancied that her hands were clenched tightly. Then Peter went to the door and the tension, if ever it had existed, had gone.

The two detectives entered; one, thickset, heavy-featured, the other, sharp and questing, his expression sour. He introduced himself briefly as Inspector Carfax of the Brittlingshire C.I.D. and his companion as Detective Sergeant Willis.

Carfax had a crisp, authoritative voice.

He looked at Roger inquiringly.

'I gather that someone has been assaulted,' he said. 'You, sir?'

'Very much so,' interposed Colonel Boon. 'Supposing I tell you what has happened, Inspector, Mr Macclesfield isn't feeling too good.'

The, story was told clearly and concisely, all drama omitted.

'I see,' said Carfax when the Colonel stopped. 'Did you recognise any of these men who attacked you, Mr Macclesfield?'

'No,' said Roger, emphatically.

'Then they weren't the same men as those who arrived by car on the cliff?'

'I don't know,' said Roger. 'I only saw one of those men, and he had a beard. I don't think I would recognise him without it.'

'Can you describe this bearded man?'

The beard; a lean, tanned hand with a scar in the middle. Carfax was greatly interested in the scar, and asked Roger to draw it from memory. Had any of them seen such a scar before? Roger, expecting an emphatic negative from each of them, was startled when Peter, who saw the drawing first, nodded calmly.

'You have!' exclaimed Angela, sitting up.

'Well, yes,' said Peter. 'And fairly often. It's a bayonet scar. At least, it's the same shape as a scar made by a bayonet—German,

I'd say. Must have gone right through the hand to make such a scar as that.'

'That's interesting,' said Carfax non-committally. He turned to Roger. 'What were you doing on the cliff?'

Roger hesitated. As the silence lengthened he thought there was a change in the detective's attitude; a coldness, which grew and became akin to hostility. It flashed through his mind that the police might think he had gone to the rock by appointment, that it hadn't been a fortuitous encounter at all. That made him hesitate still longer. Carefully looking away from Angela, he said slowly:

'I was taking a walk.'

'I see. And what time did you leave your hotel?'

'I'm staying at a boarding-house,' said Roger. 'I left about a quarter past eight.'

'Rather early, surely?' said Carfax, and now there was no questioning the suspicion in his voice.

'I suppose it was,' agreed Roger, lamely.

'Was there any particular reason for it?'

Should he tell the truth? That he had wanted to see Angela whom he had not known, that he had seen her leave early the previous morning, and hoped that she would again? No, he couldn't say that. He felt hot and confused, sure only of his throbbing head.

'I like getting up early,' he said at last, 'the morning is the best part of the day.'

'Oh,' said Carfax, his voice icy with scepticism. 'Have you walked to the rock as early as that before?'

'No, I—'

'Inspector,' interrupted Angela, 'I think Mr Macclesfield was following *me*.'

She smiled radiantly.

'Following *you*!' exclaimed Carfax.

'Weren't you, Roger?' asked Angela calmly.

Her brothers were grinning, and Colonel Boon seemed amused.

'Of course, I may be wrong,' she admitted, 'but he *has* rather—shadowed me.' Her eyes danced. 'And he was at the end of the drive this morning when I left.'

'My sister,' said Adam, 'is a siren.'

'Miss Boon's quite right,' Roger muttered.

'Thank you, Miss Boon,' Carfax said woodenly. 'Now, Mr Macclesfield, these pearls—I'd like to see them, please.'

'I'll get your coat,' said Adam. He dived into the bathroom, reappearing with the coat over his arm.

He handed it to Roger. The coat with its torn sleeve became the centre of interest. He groped for the left-hand pocket.

He was sure that the pearls were there, but no, he must have slipped them into the other pocket. But they were not there either. Flustered, he started to search all over again.

They weren't in any of the pockets.

He looked in bewilderment into Carfax's face.

'Let me see,' said Carfax in a forbidding tone, and stretched out his hand.

CHAPTER 5

THE MYSTERY

Carfax felt along the seam, and, in turn, drew out three crumpled bus tickets, the label of a packet of tobacco, two red-tipped matches, a button, a safety pin and a sixpence. With each he brought out some dark grey fluff, which he allowed to drop to the floor, although he placed each object carefully on an occasional table.

Roger found himself getting hotter and hotter. A keen dislike of Carfax leapt within him.

Satisfied that the pearls were not in that pocket, Carfax went through the others. By the time he had finished, the pile of oddments on the table had grown considerably.

The performance went on amid tense silence.

At last Carfax finished.

'Are you sure they were in that coat?' he asked disapprovingly. 'What about the one you're wearing?'

'That's mine,' said Adam. 'Have a look through it if you like, but I don't think you'll find any valuables. You'd be a very lucky man, not to say a magician, if you did. You'll have to accept the inevitable, Inspector—one of the bonny boys outside was light-fingered, and dipped quickly for the pearls when he realised that he wasn't going to get away with Roger. And Roger was too dazed to notice whether he was being robbed or not.'

'Didn't *you* notice anything?' demanded Carfax.

'I was engaged in mortal combat,' said Adam. 'That motorist had a gun.'

'You?' Carfax shot a glance at Peter—a glance loaded with suspicion and distrust.

'My dear chap!' protested Peter. 'Arms and hands and legs were flying about everywhere, not to speak of Roger falling all over the place. And as Adam has said, our main concern was to save our skins. It's a bad show, but after all—' he smiled sweetly— 'within five minutes of the clash you people were warned, so the car's almost certainly been picked up. Find the car and you'll find the pearls. Is there a reward, by the way?'

'I have no idea,' said Carfax. He looked ruffled, even angry. 'Which of you actually saw these pearls?'

'All of us except my father,' said Adam. 'And no doubt about it, they were real. Been any big robberies about here lately?'

'Until we find the pearls we can't be sure whether they were stolen,' said Carfax, reprovingly. 'They may have been smuggled into the country. I shouldn't jump to conclusions, Mr Boon.'

There was a tap at the door, and the floor-waiter entered with a laden tray of bottles and glasses. Boon, infusing some enthusiasm into his voice, invited the detectives to have a drink.

'Thank you. No,' said Carfax stiffly. 'Mr Macclesfield, it will be a help if you will put down in writing everything that happened from the moment you reached the cliffs.' He turned to go. 'Thank you for your help, Colonel Boon.'

The door closed behind him with a snap. No one moved or spoke until the last sound of footsteps had faded. To Roger it was as if everyone present was greatly relieved.

Colonel Boon went to the tray and picked up a bottle of whisky. He looked inquiringly at Roger.

'I think I'd better keep off it,' said Roger.

'I should think so,' said Angela, sharply. 'You ought to know better than to offer whisky to a man with a head like Roger's.'

'A little of what a man likes is often the best medicine,' said Colonel Boon imperturbably. He poured out three whiskies-and-soda and a gin-and-tonic, then a bitter lemon for Roger. While this was going on no one spoke; and at last each Boon solemnly lifted a glass.

'To the confounding of all policemen,' said Peter.

'To the day when my sons possess a shred of common sense,' said the Colonel, and drank. Then he held out his hand. 'Which of you has them?' he demanded.

Neither of the Boon brothers had lost their composure before, even while dealing with the three rogues outside. Now, however, they were undoubtedly discomfited. It seemed an age before Adam dropped his hand into his pocket and drew out the rope of pearls.

'Thank you,' said Colonel Boon courteously. He inspected the pearls closely, then dropped them on to the table with Roger's other possessions. 'Yes, they're real. I doubt whether we shall be able to convince Carfax that we found them outside. No doubt he and his men will search the *cul-de-sac* and probably the path along which you walked. Why on earth did you indulge in this piece of idiocy, Adam?'

'I connived at it,' Peter confessed hastily.

'I've no doubt you did,' said the Colonel drily, 'and I think without stretching a point, Carfax wasn't such a fool either. Adam, why did you do it?'

Adam fingered his beard.

'It seemed such a futile ending to hand them over to the police,' he said at last. 'Especially to such a pompous ass as Carfax.'

'A high price to pay for a little pomposity,' said his father sharply. 'I hope you realise that by this absurd antic, you've made things very difficult for Roger.'

Roger, who had been sitting in stunned silence, said faintly:

'I just don't get it.'

'Nobody could understand Adam,' contributed Angela unexpectedly, 'but he usually has some reason for what he does, even if it's a crazy one.'

'The honeyed tongue tipped with bitter aloes,' said Adam reproachfully. 'We warned you about this woman, Roger, didn't we?' he grinned light-heartedly. '*The Times*,' he cried, 'who has *The Times*?'

'It's in my bedroom, but never mind *The Times*,' said Colonel Boon. He wasn't angry; in fact he showed little but mild amusement coupled with resignation, although Roger had a feeling that there was something else, most carefully concealed. 'You've created this situation, Adam, and you've got to find a way of getting those pearls to the police.'

'Crosswords always help Adam to think,' said Angela. She slipped off the window-seat and went into one of the adjoining rooms.

Roger didn't trust himself to speak. The Boons were quite beyond him. All the men had known or guessed the truth, but no one would have dreamt of it while Carfax had been in the room. The reason for this 'absurd antic' puzzled him completely, there seemed no possible sense in it.

Angela came back with the newspaper.

'Thank you, ducky,' said Adam. He slipped into a chair and appeared to concentrate.

In less than a minute he looked up.

There was a glint in his eyes, more than a hint of excitement. He opened his lips—and then there was another tap at the door. This time there were two waiters with a trolley and a folding table. The men set about their task of laying the table with smooth dexterity, and in a few minutes they were gone.

'A hundred to one it's fish,' said Peter gloomily.

'Game,' suggested the Colonel.

It was chicken, and it was hot and appetising. All except Roger ate heartily and with pleasure, and even his appetite was not as ethereal as he expected it to be. Hardly a word was said, however, until the meal was finished and cleared away.

'And now,' said Colonel Boon, putting down his glass, 'what are the results of your brainwork, Adam? We must deliver those pearls to the police this afternoon.' This time there was a sharp note in his voice.

'I don't agree,' said Adam flatly. He met the Colonel's frown with gentle reproval. 'If only you would read the papers, father, that is, leave the political claptrap for the clowns it's written for, and concentrate on the things of interest. Listen to this.' He picked up *The Times* and began to read: '"Two thousand pounds reward for information leading to the recovery of a string of forty-two perfectly graduated high-grade pearls recently lost or stolen. Full details from *Messrs Cumfitt, Day and Dawlish*, Solicitors, Lindley House, Fleet Street, London, E.C.4."'

CHAPTER 6

£2000 REWARD OFFERED

After a short silence, the Colonel said sharply:

'Hand the paper over to me, Adam.'

'Read between the lines,' advised Adam. 'Whether you pinched 'em or found 'em you'll get the two thousand quid and no questions asked. Never mind the police, rely on the discretion of *Cumfitt, Day and Dawlish*. Ever heard of the firm, father?'

Colonel Boon shook his head.

'They've probably taken an office for this purpose,' said Peter wildly. 'It's a trap.'

'Don't be silly,' said Adam.

Angela said quietly: 'What sort of trap, Peter?'

'No reputable solicitor would put in an advertisement like that,' said Peter. 'It stinks. It *must* be a trap.' He screwed up his face into a ferocious scowl. 'It's an open invitation to the thief, if he's fool enough, to go gaily into the offices of *Cumfitt, Day and Dawlish*, tell all he knows, and then find the police waiting in the next room.'

Adam said: 'Maybe. But it's interesting. And there is a two thousand pounds reward.'

'It might not refer to these,' said the Colonel. 'Forty-two pearls, perfectly graduated. Angela—'

Angela picked up the pearls and began to count. As Roger watched the eager, vivid face, something of the tension eased from his mind.

'. . . Thirty-seven, thirty-eight, thirty-nine . . .' She was counting aloud now, and all leaned forward, their excitement growing. 'Forty . . . forty-one, forty-*two*. Roger! *Forty-two*!'

'I've heard that you often have the Devil's own job to get a reward, whether it's from an insurance company or the owners of the lost property,' said Adam calmly. 'There's almost certain to be a frenzied legal argument as to whether Roger or the police found them—that is, if we hand them over to the police. If I were in Roger's shoes I'd see *Messrs Cumfitt, Day and Dawlish*. But not alone,' he added. 'I'd take along a sturdy bodyguard, or preferably two, who would see that I wasn't battered over the head. I wouldn't take the pearls with me either, I'd think up some way of convincing the legal lads that I had the real thing, but I wouldn't hand them over until I'd got my finger on a wad of notes.'

No one spoke.

Adam gave a low-pitched, amused chuckle.

'It was a good idea while it lasted,' he said. 'But you're right. The sensible thing to do is to hand them over to the police. And since we can all weigh in with a slice of evidence, it's probable that Roger will get the reward, *if* that advertisement means what it says.'

'What an amazing name "Cumfitt" is,' said Peter. 'Almost as if it had been invented. "Day" is a pretty ordinary name certainly, but "Dawlish", now. Don't we know a Dawlish?'

'I think there's one who is an amateur detective, or something,' said Angela. 'Could it be *that* Dawlish?'

'Most unlikely, I should say. But now to proceed to the main point,' said Peter. 'Obviously Roger couldn't go up to town with Carfax watching him like a hawk. One of us would have to take 'em.'

'We mustn't get carried away again,' said the Colonel. 'A joke's a joke but it mustn't be taken too far. We must see the police. I think we'd better tell them the truth, you know.'

Silence.

'Roger,' said Angela.

There was an inflection in her voice which appeared to startle her brothers and the Colonel. And it ran through Roger, as if she had used an endearment. She looked at him with great intensity.

'*You* found them,' said Angela, 'and two thousand pounds is a lot of money. It seems a pity to risk losing it, *if* there's a chance of collecting. Besides, you needn't go up to London. If these Cumfitt people are really interested they would come down here like a shot. You could telephone them. You needn't confide your real name, but you could make an appointment with them somewhere—say, at the rock where it happened. The point is, Roger—' She paused.

'Yes?' said Roger slowly.

'Don't be bullied by any of the Boons,' advised Angela. 'Make up your own mind and do what you think's best.'

'All very winsome,' said the Colonel drily. 'Roger, if I were you, I'd rest for an hour or two on your own. You'll feel better then, and you can give the matter proper thought. Angela is right in so far as we can probably find a way of getting round the difficulty with the police—if you decide it's worth it. We'll go out, and leave you here for an hour or two. I'll see the pearls safely into the manager's safe.'

The armchair was very comfortable, and the state of Roger's head precluded any possibility of concentrated thinking. He was in a mood, in fact, which lent itself to daydreams, and the threat of further violence which overhung him seemed distant and vague. Angela, counting the pearls, was a vision which he was likely to retain for a long time. Two thousand pounds floated before him rather appealingly. Two thousand pounds—Angela—this strange, poised, friendly family—it would be good to become part of it. He felt as if he had known all of them for years.

Two thousand pounds.

Come to think of it, it was almost a fortune. He recalled a strange disquiet, a feeling that even among the Boons there was an undercurrent of tension, which appeared now and again. It might have been fancy; but he couldn't entirely dismiss it from his mind.

Was there someone creeping about the room? Was he imagining the soft stealthiness of concealed movement? He half-opened his eyes, but could only see the curtains, drawn at the windows, and the front of another armchair. So he had been asleep. His mouth was parched, his head stiff—and he was frightened. Had the men discovered where he was, and come back?

A door slowly opened.

He looked towards it without opening his eyes any further, and saw the shadow of a man or a woman on the carpet. Gradually it lengthened as whoever it was came slowly forward.

His knuckles whitened on the arms of his chair.

He must feign sleep, wait until whoever it was drew nearer, and then spring. He mustn't allow himself to be knocked about again. He—

It was Angela!

She appeared suddenly, smiling a rather secret smile as she looked at him.

He stirred, and opened his eyes wide, blinking dazedly in the strong light.

'Did I wake you? I didn't mean—'

'No, I was only dozing.'

She sat on the arm of the nearest chair.

'Feeling better?'

'I'm terribly thirsty.'

'We'll have tea very soon,' Angela promised him. 'The others sent me up to see if you were awake. They're having tea downstairs. I've ordered yours to be served here.'

Roger said: 'I can't act the invalid any longer.'

'Oh, nonsense! None of us would have missed this for the world. Especially Daddy, although he pretends to be disapproving, and the champion of common sense.'

Roger gave a dry little laugh.

'You're an uncommon family,' he remarked.

'We do take a bit of getting used to,' admitted Angela. She paused, and then said abruptly: 'I'm worried about you.'

'Then it's time you stopped worrying,' said Roger. 'I am quite capable of looking after myself, in spite of evidence to the contrary.'

'What's Cliff Terrace like?'

'Pleasant enough, and the food's fairly good. I think I was lucky to get in there.'

'I don't mean like that, I mean could those men break in easily?'

'No more easily than anywhere else,' said Roger. 'You really needn't worry about me. I'll leave the pearls here,' he added. 'Your father won't mind that, will he?'

'Of course not. But hang the pearls! It's you I'm worried about. You don't even know your assailants, do you?'

That remark shook him; it was tantamount to asking whether he had told the police the truth! He returned her gaze grimly.

Through his mind flooded a simple truth. He had taken the Boons and their trust in him for granted. Now—was it possible that Angela had been sent to pump him? That they suspected him of lying?

It was an uncomfortable thought.

'Well, I didn't know them,' he said gruffly.

'So you said,' said Angela. 'I—Oh, here's the tea.'

Over tea, he decided he had been absurdly touchy. And although Angela didn't ask directly, he knew that she was dying to know whether he had decided what to do about *Cumfitt's*. He didn't tell her that he hadn't yet given the matter any serious thought; but he could tell that she hoped he would follow her suggestion. There wouldn't be much harm in it, surely. A telephone call, a rendezvous, and afterwards they would probably know much more than they did now, and be able to decide what to do.

He leaned his head back, smiling rather complacently, because she was now obviously hanging on his words.

'I wonder if there's a London telephone directory in the hotel,' he added musingly.

She jumped up.

'To find *Cumfitt's* number?'

'I think I might—' began Roger.

'It's Temple Bar 0891,' cried Angela. 'I've looked it up. And we've agreed that the rock *is* the right place. We had a look round there this afternoon. Oh, and Adam found your pipe,' she added, and hurried into the bedroom, coming out in a flash with the pipe in her hand. 'The telephone's just behind you.'

Fool! Of course she'd never doubted him.

CHAPTER 7

THE RENDEZVOUS

The following evening, when dusk was gathering, Roger approached the rock, his pipe in his mouth, his head bare and no longer aching. He told himself that he was as fit as he had been when he had walked along this path in Angela's wake, and, in spite of his tension about the forthcoming meeting with the man from *Cumfitt's* he smiled at the recollection.

There were few people about, for it was nearly half-past seven, time when most holiday-makers were having their evening meal, and the cliffs were nearly deserted. Three or four couples were lying here and there on the grass, and a man with long, brown legs, wearing khaki shorts and carrying a rucksack on his back, was staring out to sea. A tandem cycle stood near the hedge which bordered the path across which the car had come.

Roger knew that Angela and her brothers were somewhere near at hand, but he could not see them. The Colonel had decided to stay at the hotel.

Roger went to the edge of the cliff and sat down—as he had arranged with the man to whom he had spoken on the telephone.

He had shown no surprise when Roger had suggested a rendez-vous, agreeing readily to the meeting-place.

Now that he was actually here, Roger wished he hadn't said 'sitting'. He would feel much more secure if he were standing up a few yards from the edge. But nothing could be done about that now.

The hiker hitched up his rucksack and strode off towards Brittling. The wind whipped along the surface of the grass with unpleasant sharpness.

Roger ran over the details of the appointment. The man from *Cumfitt, Day and Dawlish* was to approach him from Brittling, and say 'Are you Mr Curtis?' And Roger was to get up and answer 'Yes, have you come from London?' To which the man would reply 'From Fleet Street, to be precise.' It sounded silly and melodramatic, but would serve his purpose.

Two people were approaching from Brittling, and he hadn't been told to expect two. No one else was in sight, but by now it was so gloomy that he could see no more than a couple of hundred yards away. He looked at his watch: it wanted two minutes to the half-hour, the time of the appointment.

Roger started to refill his pipe. His hands weren't very steady. Apart from the man who was coming to see him, there might be others very much interested. The uncertainty, the impossibility of guessing what might happen next, was wearing.

Twenty-five minutes to eight; and no one approached him. Twenty minutes to. Confound it, the fellow was late, it was too bad. Now, too, the folly of what he was doing came home to him. Crazy fool! He should never have listened to Angela or her brothers, he ought to have known that the only sensible thing was to hand the pearls over to the police. Two thousand pounds weren't picked up so easily as this! Supposing Peter was right, and the advertisement was a police trap.

Roger shivered.

It was a quarter to eight, and he could only just see the dial of his watch. A cigarette glowed to his right, but he could no longer pick out the couples. He heard a girl giggle and caught the name Freddie. But how could one differentiate between shadows which were lovers and shadows which might hold menace?

A woman screamed!

The cry broke the quiet of the night as sharply as a glass breaking. Roger started to his feet. There was a lull—ominous, menacing—and then the giggling girl said 'Freddie, what was that?' There came another scream, followed by Adam's unmistakable voice:

'Angela! Where—'

'Look out!' That was Peter.

The voices came from the left. Roger ran towards them, passing a couple who were scrambling to their feet. Then came a flash of light, followed by the sharp report of a shot!

Another shot rang out.

'*Freddie!*' shrieked the giggling girl. 'Freddie!'

'Angela!' That was Adam again. 'Are you all right? Where—'

His voice was cut off by the sudden sound of a motor cycle starting up.

'*Angela!*' roared Adam.

A red light glowed not far away. It was heading along the cliff path, away from Brittling.

The beam of a powerful torch shot out. It caught the rider, and a girl, flung over the front of the machine. There was no mistaking that tawny hair, which nearly swept the ground. But the torchlight shone on something else—a crumpled body, near the hedge where the motor-cycle had been hidden.

Roger was now only a few yards from Adam.

'Adam! Did you see—'

'Only too well. My God, if they hurt Angela, I'll—'

Adam broke off. Roger stared in anguish after the red light. There was the driver, heading away from the town, without a light to guide him, perhaps already perilously near the edge of the cliff. One false turn of the handlebars and the machine would be over.

'Lend me a hand, will you?' asked Adam, and he put the torch on the ground so that it shone on Peter's huddled figure. There was an ugly red gash on the latter's head, and he looked white and ill. Adam took off his coat and rolled it into a pillow, and they rested Peter's head on it.

'Can—can we help?' a man asked timidly from a little way behind them.

'Very good of you,' said Adam. 'I don't think there's much you can do.' He stood up, undecided—it was a rare thing to see a Boon unable to make up his mind. 'There's no one here with a bicycle, I suppose?' he added hopefully.

The man who had offered help was silent; but another couple, Freddie and his girl-friend, drew near—and Freddie said that they had a tandem. Adam at once grew decisive and brisk. He scribbled a note, which he asked the couple to take to Colonel Boon, and Roger did not question the wisdom of going first to the Colonel and leaving it to him to deal with the police. Adam, satisfied that a decision had been taken, bent down by his brother's side.

'What have you said to your father?' Roger asked.

'Asked for a car or an ambulance, and a search to be started for that motor-cycle,' said Adam bitterly.

Roger didn't answer—he seemed fated to play a silent part when with the Boons. He felt furiously angry because this ghastly ending to the plan was his fault, and yet it was not directly due to him. But he should have known better than to have been argued into it.

Adam plucked at his arm.

'A word in your ear before the fireworks begin. First, don't blame yourself. Our fault. Mine, primarily. And you were one against three, with one neutral. Get that clear. And this is even more important. Say nothing about the pearls. We came out here for a walk; Angela and Peter tried to get down the side of the cliff and were coming up when they were attacked. If there's any question as to why we split up you can say there was a quarrel between you and the rest of us. Or at least a difference. All clear?'

'It certainly isn't,' said Roger heavily.

'Now, Roger—'

'And "now Roger" won't stop me this time,' said Roger, on the point of real anger. 'I was prepared to take a chance over the pearls, but when it comes to Angela—'

'Exactly. Mustn't take a chance with Angela.'

'So we'll tell the police everything,' declared Roger.

'You aren't seeing it straight, old chap,' reasoned Adam. 'Nasty gang of crooks involved in this. Murderous devils, who want the pearls. They think you have them—or we have them—and they'll offer Angela in exchange. If we tell Carfax about the pearls, he'll take them, and we'll have nothing then to barter for Angela.'

Roger was silent.

'See what I mean?' asked Adam. 'Daren't take the risk of delivering up the pearls now, they're our one hope. My father will agree about this,' he added, as if that clinched the matter. 'At least wait until you've had a chat with him.'

And Roger agreed to wait.

A police-car followed by an ambulance came jerking along the cliff-top. It was comparatively simple to tell them the agreed version of the story. The police-car was equipped with walkie-talkie radio, and flashed details to headquarters. Then Peter was put into the ambulance, and Roger and Adam rode with him, accompanied by a silent, rather sullen constable.

Peter was taken straight to the hospital. Then Roger, Adam, and the silent policeman went on to the police station. It was a bleak building, cold and inhospitable. A large, bulky man questioned them closely. He knew about the earlier incidents, and made no attempt to hide his doubts about the truth of what they now told him. Roger was with him for half an hour, and was questioned with a chilling thoroughness which increased his respect for the Brittling police, but failed to break his story. Then Adam was put through the same ordeal, and it was nearly ten o'clock before they were allowed to leave.

Colonel Boon said little; but when Roger left, just before midnight, he was convinced that it was right to hold on to the pearls, which were still in the safe at the *Bay Hotel*.

Adam having seen him off to Cliff Terrace, which was only ten minutes' walk away from the hotel, he strode quickly down the main drive towards the promenade. He had not gone far before he knew that someone was following him.

He crossed the deserted road and stood looking down at the sea, which was only dimly visible, the man behind him walking stolidly in his wake. There was nothing furtive about the fellow, and with a sickening sense of alarm, Roger realised that he was probably a policeman. Yet there was an edge of danger, and when he turned up a narrow side street, his heart began to thump. It was very dark here. But his shadower did not quicken his pace, and by the time he reached the top of the hill Roger felt rather glad of his company. For out of the darkness a man might spring without any warning; it had been mere bravado to come here alone, he should have accepted the Colonel's invitation to stay at the hotel, using Peter's room.

He reached 14, Cliff Terrace, and took out his key. The house was in darkness. His follower stood on the other side of the road, a vague black shape. Roger went in and closed the door, then switched on a light. These were tall houses, and his room was on the fourth floor. He switched on the lights as he went up, for all of them could be switched off again from the top landing.

It was very quiet.

He switched off the downstairs lights, stepped into his room, and pressed down that switch.

Nothing happened.

He stood quite still, with his fingers on the switch. He could see the window faintly outlined against the sky; it rattled suddenly under a gust of wind. The draught took the door out of his hand, and it slammed behind him. At first he could hear nothing but the beating of his own heart. He stood quite still until that quietened.

Someone else was breathing in here.

He lost the sound in another flurry of alarm—and then saw a dark figure rise from a chair in the corner. A man spoke in a quiet, casual voice.

'Are you Mr Curtis?' he asked.

CHAPTER 8

THE MAN FROM CUMFITT'S

Curtis!

The rigmarole which Roger had learned by heart came back to him as if someone had pressed a button. As his mind cleared, so did his attitude towards the dark shape of the speaker.

The shadow repeated: '*Are* you Mr Curtis?'

'Yes,' said Roger quietly. 'Have you come from London?'

'From Fleet Street, to be precise,' said the shadow.

There was a sound, as of metal on metal—and then the light came on. Roger saw a gigantic fellow stretching up without difficulty to see that the lamp was firmly fastened into the point.

Roger surveyed the stranger—and in spite of himself he could not prevent a slight fluttering of nerves. Had this man showed signs of hostility anyone would have been justified in feeling afraid, for his size owed nothing to tricks of light and shadow. He towered above Roger, who was nearly six feet tall.

'Mind if I smoke?' the man asked, and flicked a lighter.

'I come from *Cumfitt's*.'

'There is a detective outside,' said Roger quietly. He hoped that would shake the fellow, for he was tired of being caught at a disadvantage; but the other did not turn a hair.

'So I gathered,' he said. 'A detective, you may like to know, by the name of Willis. Strong and silent.'

If this were how the conversation was going to turn Roger determined to keep his end up. The fellow had at least succeeded in clearing his mind of anxieties and fears, even of indignation.

'You telephoned *Cumfitt's* and gave a false name,' the big man said pleasantly.

'You didn't turn up for the rendezvous, and I'd very much like to break your neck,' answered Roger, not pleasantly at all.

The giant chuckled.

'Well, try,' he invited—and his grin was so expansive and beguiling that Roger's grim face broke into a smile. 'That's better,' went on the stranger. 'After all, we may as well be friends if we're going to do business together.'

'How did you know where to find me?' Roger asked.

'Oh, that was easy enough. We were already interested in you, because of your interviews with Carfax and the fact that you've been knocked for six once or twice. In short, my spies are at work,' the stranger added with another infectious grin. '*Do* you know where the pearls are?' he demanded.

'Possibly.'

The other said abruptly: 'What on earth made you get mixed up with this mob?'

'I'm not mixed up with any mob,' said Roger spiritedly. 'I've never seen any of them before.'

'I know that's what you told Carfax,' said the other. 'But I can take something stronger. And the truth will be safe with me. Isn't it something like this? You joined with Mizzy's mob and they wouldn't share out, so you lifted the pearls and tried to dispose of them on your own. So Mizzy came after you. Now what could be simpler than that?'

'I am not, and never have been, a member of Mizzy's mob,' said Roger, steadily. 'I found those pearls.'

'Found?' It was satisfying to have startled this man.

'Found,' repeated Roger. 'And, having read your advertisement, I decided to get in touch with you personally, instead of through the police.'

'I'm almost inclined to believe you. But what's gone wrong?'

'When I know more about you, and why you want the pearls, I might tell you.'

'Right. Well, for a start, my name is Dawlish. Not the third partner in *Cumfitt, Day and Dawlish*, by the way. I am the Patrick Dawlish who, from time to time, presumes to step in where the police fear to tread. This is such an occasion. Of late there have been a number of jewel robberies of some consequence. Among those robbed was a close friend of mine. At his request, and with the faint approval—or rather, without the active disapproval—of Scotland Yard, I agreed to help. You see, I know quite a bit about Mizzy's mob. Hence the advertisement in *The Times*, using as an accommodation address the office of a relative who strongly disapproves, yet agreed to help.'

Roger, having lit his pipe, glanced through the little puffs of smoke at Dawlish. There had been a convincing ring in the big man's voice, and the story had been told smoothly; either it was true or most carefully rehearsed.

'Not convinced?' asked Dawlish.

'Not entirely.'

'Hmm,' murmured Dawlish, 'an awkward young man. Have the Boons anything to do with it?' he shot out suddenly.

'What do you know about the Boons?' snapped Roger.

'Ah,' exclaimed Dawlish. 'So that's it.' He looked at Roger keenly. '*Now* I'm beginning to understand.'

'And what do you understand?' asked Roger heatedly.

Dawlish waved a conciliatory finger.

'Oh, this and that. A friend of a friend of mine knows Colonel Boon,' he explained, 'and will undoubtedly give me the necessary reference. And, judging from the mulish look on your face, you're not going to talk freely until you're assured of my *bona fides*, so I suppose the best thing is to call it a day.' He stood up quickly. 'I'm staying at the *Bay Hotel*, so in the morning I can be picked up as a hotel acquaintance, and the watchful eyes of the hotel detective, who is undoubtedly hand-in-glove with Carfax, will be deceived. Satisfy you?' he added.

He didn't speak of the pearls again, and appeared to be quite content to wait until the morning. Nothing else could have weakened Roger's suspicions of him so quickly. Besides, he wanted all the help he could get for Angela.

'Please sit down again,' he said. 'I've decided to talk to you.'

Without a word Dawlish sank back into his chair, and Roger began his story a little incoherently; first relating what had happened on the cliff, and then going back to the beginning. After twenty minutes there was very little that Dawlish did not know.

The first comment he made was:

'Adam Boon's quite right. Mizzy will almost certainly offer Angela in exchange for the pearls. But Mizzy—' He broke off, his expression bleak. It filled Roger with alarm, and there was an edge to his voice as he demanded:

'What were you going to say?'

'You are very fond of this Angela, aren't you?' asked Dawlish quietly.

'What has that got to do with it?' demanded Roger.

'It will make a difference,' said Dawlish. 'Mizzy has a way with women. And a most unpleasant reputation.'

Roger felt sick.

Dawlish said gently: 'There's one thing. Carfax may not be a genial personality, but he's extremely efficient. By now the Yard will know all about Angela Boon's disappearance, and there will be a countrywide search moving by the morning. On the other hand, there is the motor-boat.'

'What's that got to do with it?'

'Plenty, I'm afraid. Mizzy obviously sends some of the stuff he steals out of the country by sea—and a motor-boat can take a passenger or two as well as a load of loot.'

Roger sat quite still.

'And all we have to play with are the pearls,' went on Dawlish musingly. 'The one good thing is that Mizzy obviously wants those pearls pretty badly, or he wouldn't have tried to get them from you in the middle of Brittling. He seldom gets as bold as daylight robbery. Odd,' added Dawlish, rubbing his forefinger along the bridge of his nose. 'He's usually very careful, and you wouldn't call his antics careful today, would you? Holdup in the car, and then the daring job on the motor-cycle. Yes, he wants those pearls desperately. That's interesting in itself, especially when he's been careless enough to lose them.' He thought about this for a moment, drumming his fingers against the arm of the chair, then shot Roger another of his keen, penetrating glances. 'Prepared to exchange those pearls for the girl?' he demanded abruptly.

CHAPTER 9

WET DAY

The rain which had been threatening since early evening came during the night. When Roger awoke from a restless sleep it was lashing against the window. The wild fury of the elements matched his frame of mind, but his was an impotent fury, because there was nothing he could do.

Dawlish had left, after putting that one significant question and receiving an answer which must have satisfied even him. The question was clear in Roger's mind as he drank a cup of tea brought up to him by Mr Webber, a meek, drooping-moustached man who as husband of the proprietress of the house was its theoretical master.

Meek he might be, but he was also—when away from his wife—exceptionally garrulous. A shrill call from the lower regions recalling him at last, Roger leapt thankfully from his bed, bathed, shaved, despatched a fairly generous breakfast and had left the house within an hour.

Wind and rain drove into his face, and it was unpleasantly cold. Even here, a quarter of mile from the sea, he could hear the breakers roaring.

Roger turned into the main drive of the *Bay Hotel*, and saw a uniformed policeman, his cape glistening, standing near the wall. So not only himself, but the *Bay Hotel* was being watched. Perhaps the Boon family had come under suspicion. But surely the police would not suspect them!

As he approached the Boons' door he hesitated; what could he say to Adam and the Colonel? How were they feeling after a night which must have been filled with anxiety?

He tapped on the door of the sitting-room; there was no answer. He tapped again, and then tried the handle, but the door was locked. He was filled with even deeper misgivings; they had seen him come, and did not want to talk to him. Could he wonder if they hated the sight of him, and wished that he had never appeared?

The floor waiter, approaching with a breakfast tray, looked at him with some surprise.

'Colonel Boon? But they've gone, sir—left this morning, unexpectedly I understand.'

Roger looked stupidly at the man, and then with a muttered 'Oh, thanks,' turned on his heel. It was—fantastic! Hang it, Peter was still in hospital, they wouldn't desert him.

He slowed down as he neared the reception desk. The clerk was at the telephone, and the register was open on the desk. Roger could see the Boon signatures, but not that of Patrick Dawlish. Had he lied—or was he staying at the hotel under another name?

The receptionist replaced the receiver and turned to him.

'Can I help you?'

'Er—yes. Colonel Boon—'

'He has been called away, and left this morning,' said the girl briskly.

'Did he leave a message for me? My name is Macclesfield.'

'No, there was no message.'

'A forwarding address?'

'We had no special instructions.' The girl's voice was polite but chilling. 'If you wish a letter to be forwarded we will post it to his last known address.'

'Thanks,' said Roger. He was turning away when he suddenly remembered the pearls. He said sharply: 'Colonel Boon left a packet here yesterday—it was to be put in the manager's safe. Can you tell me whether he collected it?'

'Presumably, yes,' said the girl.

'Let me see the manager, please,' said Roger curtly.

The girl looked at him for the first time with interest, and beckoned a pageboy. 'Take this gentleman to the manager's office, Cedric.'

Roger followed him.

The pearls were gone; the Boons were gone; and Dawlish had never been here. He faced those facts grimly. It was almost a waste of time to see the manager, for he was quite sure what the answer would be. And if he were right, what should he do next?

The manager, immaculate in black coat and striped trousers, was a small, pale man with glinting blue eyes. He put himself at Mr Macclesfield's service. Ah—Colonel Boon. Mr Macclesfield should understand that it was a confidential matter but—yes, a packet had been left in the safe for a few hours. A few *hours*, Roger echoed. It had been taken out after dinner the previous evening by Colonel Boon himself. The manager dropped his voice and waved his hands deprecatingly. He hoped he would be forgiven if he asked a question: what was Mr Macclesfield's interest in the packet?

'Oh, just that of a friend of Colonel Boon,' said Roger.

Roger thanked the manager and left the hotel in a state of

inward agitation. How could he explain this disappearance without becoming suspicious—and that was a mild word—of Colonel Boon?

A gust of wind nearly swept Roger off his feet, and this time his hat went flying. He turned and staggered after it. A car was coming towards him, but he paid it no attention. The wind frisked his hat away tantalisingly, yard by yard. He caught it with difficulty. As he did so he saw the car slowing down.

The driver's door opened—and Dawlish grinned at him.

'Like a lift?' The stentorian voice was only just audible above the crash of waves. 'Come on!'

'No!' roared Roger.

'You'll be sorry if you don't. Come on!'

As he spoke Roger became aware of a stranger bearing down upon him—a stranger whose head was also bared to the rain. He shot out a hand.

'For your own good!' Dawlish shouted.

Next moment Roger was bundled headfirst into the car.

CHAPTER 10

QUICK CHANGE

Too breathless to speak, Roger fell into the back seat. The car passed the head of the deserted pier and the *Mary Anne*, then swept along a road on the right. Roger couldn't see the speedometer, but he suspected that they were travelling at over fifty miles an hour.

In no time at all they had passed the boundary of Brittling and were heading for the open country. Roger became unpleasantly conscious of the exceeding discomfort of rain trickling from his hair to his neck. He was rather ineffectually mopping with an already soaked handkerchief when Dawlish's companion spoke.

'You'll find a towel behind you.'

After a moment's hesitation—does one thank one's virtual abductor?—Roger gave a muttered acknowledgement, found the towel and rubbed vigorously.

A stationary car loomed up in front of them.

'Ah,' said Dawlish, and raised his voice. 'We're going to change cars, Macclesfield; don't be awkward.'

The big car slowed down and pulled up immediately behind a smaller one, which stood beneath a row of beech trees. Through the side window Roger saw that a woman sat at the wheel. Dawlish opened his door and climbed out; his companion followed him.

A third man appeared from the stationary car, and as the rain lashed about them they held a brief conversation. Finally, he took the wheel of Dawlish's car, while Dawlish, his companion and Roger crowded into the second.

'And that reminds me,' said Dawlish airily. 'Roger Macclesfield, my wife.'

Both Roger and Mrs Dawlish murmured 'How do you do' at the same time, then smiled spontaneously.

Dawlish said: 'I think perhaps a word of explanation is due.' He turned to Roger. 'The police were watching you very closely, and we thought it better that you should keep away from them for a bit.'

'You might consult me about that next time,' said Roger. He spoke sharply, but there was no conviction in his annoyance. To his own surprise, he did not really feel annoyed; Dawlish and his friends affected him in much the same way as the Boons had. 'Where are we going?'

'My wife, who is capable of anything, found us a country cottage,' said Dawlish. 'So we're going there to dry off and generally cope with the situation. Incidentally,' he added, 'my wife never helps me in such affairs as this unless she's convinced it's in a good cause.'

'Very reassuring,' said Roger. 'I hope you'll be able to convince *me*. Why weren't you at the *Bay Hotel*?'

'We were,' said Dawlish, 'but not under our own name. And we decided to move on quickly.'

Roger was only slightly mollified.

'I suppose you realise that the police will almost certainly assume that I've run away from them?'

'Well, you haven't committed any crime—or have you?' asked Dawlish mildly.

'They'll probably assume that I have.'

'My dear chap, the police have to assume something,' said Dawlish. 'Shall we talk at the cottage?'

'No,' said Roger. 'Now. Are you serious when you say that you brought me away because the police were following me?'

'Yes,' said Dawlish. 'You see, you're rather an innocent in this affair. I think it's likely that Mizzy will only deal with you, as he probably thinks that you still have the pearls. And that means that you've become extremely important, even though you know nothing about it.'

'Try putting it in words of three letters,' said Roger drily.

'Well, to begin with, Mizzy wants those pearls. And he's offered a deal—the pearls for Angela Boon. I doubt if he'll play, except with you as the go-between. So we had to get you away from the eagle eye of the police. Get it?'

Roger said slowly: 'Yes, but—'

'You haven't the pearls, I know,' said Dawlish patiently. 'On the other hand, I think we shall soon be able to catch up with Colonel Boon. Quick flit of the Colonel's, wasn't it? He's possibly anxious to get the pearls away, knowing their value as a bargaining weapon. All in all, I thought it would be better if we got to the cottage and had a bath and change before we started discussing the situation.'

They turned off the main road with a swoop, and Roger caught sight of the name '*Valcoombe*' on a signpost. Now they were in real country, with winding lanes, thatched cottages, and Norman churches surrounded by sloping and embedded tombstones. They came at last to a white gate leading to a rough drive.

In fair weather, with the blue sky behind it and the sun

shining, the cottage before them would have looked delightful. Even now it was not unattractive.

Mrs Dawlish pulled up outside the porch.

'I think I'd better put the car away first,' said Dawlish. 'No—you hop out, no point in you getting wet—and we'll walk back from the garage.'

'Right. Don't be long.'

As Mrs Dawlish climbed out Roger saw her face for the first time. He had gained the impression of someone of unusual beauty. He saw now that though that was not factually true, the impression would be for him, and for most people, lasting. Dawlish slid into her seat and drove towards the garage, which was twenty yards from the cottage itself.

'I don't think there's a ghost of a chance of anyone knowing where we are, and we certainly need a breathing-space. And that reminds me—the chap you've been sitting next to is Cedric Forbes. A much heartier worthy than he looks.'

Forbes grinned.

They were standing at the door of the garage looking at a dismal prospect of wet trees, bent grass and a hawthorn hedge.

'Well, let's get to the house, instead of blathering here,' Forbes said, and, buttoning his coat about him, lowered his head and charged forward.

When Dawlish and Roger reached the porch he was pulling at an old-fashioned pull-type bell, which was clanging noisily.

'And now she's shut the door and is going to keep us waiting on the doorstep,' he complained. 'You'll have to do something about Felicity, Pat. It's me or she. Or is it her or I?—well, it's one of us,' he added aggrievedly, and tugged at the bell again.

The clanging note faded.

'She's probably lighting a fire,' said Dawlish, frowning. 'But it's odd—why didn't she leave the door open for us?'

'The perversity of woman,' said Forbes, raising his eyes to the top of the porch. A drop of water splashed on to the tip of his nose, and he backed away hastily. Roger grinned, and Dawlish said unfeelingly:

'Serves you right.' He raised his voice. 'Fel!'

The door remained shut.

'Have you *tried* the door?' Roger asked suddenly.

Forbes turned the handle and pushed, and the door opened. He burst out laughing.

'Now that's what I call typical feminine deceit! She did it just to make a fool of me. You wait until I set eyes on you, Felicity.'

He pushed the door wide open.

A man stood in front of them, holding an automatic in his right hand. A tall, bearded man.

CHAPTER 11

THE SHOCK

The shock of alarm which ran through Roger was the greater because he recognised this man: he it was who had asked him for a light on the cliff. Behind him, halfway down the stairs, was a second man similarly armed.

Roger glanced round.

Two men were in sight in front of the cottage. Each had been sheltering behind a tree, and each held a carbine.

Roger stepped across the threshold, his hands held just above his head. Forbes and Dawlish followed.

The bearded man said sharply: 'Upstairs, Dawlish. And keep your hands high.'

Roger expected Dawlish to refuse; to make some effort to turn the tables. But instead he went to the foot of the stairs and began to mount them. Forbes followed.

'In here,' said the bearded man. Stepping towards the right, he kicked open a door.

It led into a long, narrow room, charmingly furnished, with flowered chintzes at the windows and loose covers on chairs and sofa. It was a homely room, with an old, friendly-looking chiming clock on the mantelpiece with a coloured and decorated dial.

An odd background, thought Roger, for a gunman and his gang.

The bearded man said: 'Now you know how much help you can expect from Dawlish.' There was a sneer in his voice. 'You were a fool to have anything to do with him. *Now* you're going to deal with us.'

Roger said: 'What about?'

'The pearls, Macclesfield. Where are the pearls?'

Roger didn't answer.

The bearded man raised a menacing fist, but before it could fall Roger struck out, and more by luck than judgement caught the man on the nose. His captor shot out a foot, kicking him viciously in the groin.

Roger gasped and doubled up.

Gradually—very gradually—the pain became bearable. His captor caught him by the coat collar, pulled him to his feet and then shoved him into the chair.

'Where are the pearls?' he demanded.

Roger moistened his lips.

'Want some more?' demanded the bearded man. 'Or would you rather we beat up one of the women?'

One! Did that mean that Angela was here? Roger gripped the arms of the chair and stared into the man's face. He could see now the lines of cruelty, and ruthlessness. He did not think there was much doubt that this was 'Mizzy' or that he would carry out his threat if that was the way to get what he wanted.

'Where are the pearls?' the man repeated, and struck him again. This time it was a blow with clenched fists.

He saw the bearded man grinning—but not at him; he was

looking at the door, the open door, where a woman—a girl—stood on the threshold, with a man behind her.

Angela!

Her glance swept swiftly round the room and settled on Roger.

'Macclesfield—' the voice was harsher now, with an ugly undertone—'where are those pearls?'

Had Roger known where to find the pearls he would have said so then, but a new horror was added to the rest. He didn't know, and it was more than unlikely that this man would believe him.

The bearded man's eyes, sadistic, glittering, were very near his own.

'I don't know,' said Roger desperately, 'they were taken out of the hotel safe last night—I don't know where they are.'

There was a moment of indecision—as if his tone half-convinced the other that he was telling the truth.

He said slowly, each word heavy with menace: 'Who took them?'

Roger was silent.

'*Who took them?*'

'I don't see why you shouldn't tell him,' said Angela calmly. 'Was it my father?'

'Yes,' said Roger dully. 'I'd given him the pearls and he was to put them in the hotel safe, but it appears that he left the hotel unexpectedly and took them with him. I just don't know where they are. I wish to heaven I'd never seen the damn things!' he added fervently.

'So Boon took them away, did he?' The man plucked at his beard, and the scar showed again. 'It's about time I knew what your father is up to,' he added, turning to Angela. 'Suppose you tell me?'

'There is nothing more I can tell you,' said Angela quietly.

'We'll see. It's surprising how much you remember when it's going to hurt if you forget. Take her out,' he ordered the man at the door.

'Angela!' exclaimed Roger. 'Don't—'

He was going to say, 'Don't hold out,' but he didn't finish, because the bearded man struck him across the face.

The door closed, the key turned in the lock, and Roger found himself alone.

In the grounds beneath the tree the man with a carbine stood, watchful, unmoving.

The house was silent.

CHAPTER 12

THE RESOURCE OF PATRICK DAWLISH

Meanwhile Dawlish and Forbes had been forced, at the point of a gun, up a narrow loft-ladder, to the attic. No one, hearing Dawlish exchanging airy persiflage with Forbes would have guessed that he was fully aware of the dangerous spot he was in.

As Dawlish reached the hatch-doors Felicity leaned over the edge to help him up. So, this was where they had put her. Relief that they would now be together battled with anxiety at the danger which undoubtedly faced them.

As Forbes climbed up behind him, the guards banged and bolted the hatch-doors, leaving them in almost total darkness.

There was a click—and then a thin pencil of light shone out from Dawlish's small pocket-torch. They stood together, looking round the walls—and what the torchlight revealed was not reassuring. Cobwebs draped the corners and hung from the sloping roof.

The floor was filthy. In one corner was an old packing-case, the sides gaping open. Near this they could see a clothes'-horse, a dilapidated child's high-chair, two suitcases and a pile of yellowed newspapers.

The torch went out.

'Can't waste the battery,' said Dawlish briefly. 'There is only that, and a box of about a dozen matches, between us and total darkness.'

By feeling, and the brief light of an occasional match, they dragged out the suitcases and sat on them.

'Looks as if we're sunk,' said Forbes gloomily. 'There's nothing to prevent them reinforcing those bolts, so that we can't open the hatch, and leaving us here for ever. And to think,' he added, 'that you let me help you in this little job! Let's have a look at the roof, old chap. Just one match,' he pleaded. 'How many have you got left?'

'Ten.'

'Ten—little—matches,' Forbes began to sing, 'lying in a box. Ten—little—matches, lying in a box. If one little maa-atch should accidentally strike, there'll be nine little match-es— lying in a box! Round song,' he added sonorously. 'Now all together—'

'Keep singing,' whispered Dawlish urgently.

'Ten—little—matches
Lying in a box!
Ten little matches
Lying in a box!
If one of the little matches
Should accidentally strike
There'll be nine little matches,
Lying in a box!'

They were at the end of the second stanza when a match struck, stabbing the dark. Dawlish was near the wall, peering at the ceiling, prodding the webbed and dusty rafters.

He eased away a few loose tiles; not too far, for if one fell it might attract the attention of the guards in the grounds.

Nevertheless, a faint glimmer of grey daylight spread about the loft.

The round-song came to an end, and Forbes started on 'One Man and his Dog'.

'Any chance of making a hole big enough for me to climb through?' he sang.

'Yes,' said Dawlish, 'but they're watching the roof. And they'd take pot shots at you.'

'Well, I'm not very big,' muttered Forbes, at the end of the first verse. 'They might miss, and I could run like hell to the village for an A.A. box, and have help here in no time.'

'I don't think any of us will go just yet,' said Dawlish. 'I— Hallo, there's a roof-light. Wait a moment.'

Something tore.

More light came into the loft, and now it was possible for them to see everywhere.

'Any ideas, Pat?'

'Plenty,' said Dawlish. 'But a long way from foolproof. We want one of us to get outside, preferably you, as you can shin down a drainpipe better than most. But they've got those men in the grounds and, as I've said, they'll be watching the roof. Therefore distraction is needed. There isn't an old bucket about, is there?'

'There's an enamel pot over there,' said Felicity.

She reached the high-chair, and slid the pot from its fastening. It was of white enamel, badly chipped.

Dawlish's expression showed the utmost satisfaction.

'It's just what we want. We ought to start the fire near the hatch.'

'*Fire*?' exclaimed Forbes, allowing the lustiness of his singing to wobble into silence.

'You blow the smoke through the cracks in the hatch-door, and so raise the alarm,' said Dawlish, patiently.

Forbes said: 'Oh, yes, of course. You light the fire, I blow. Fine.' He looked at Dawlish darkly. 'Have a rest, old chap. Try the cot.'

'But I'm serious,' repeated Dawlish.

'Oh,' said Forbes. 'Pity. Let me tell you about a fire I once saw. All started from a cigarette end, and the fire-engine couldn't get there in time to save the poor blighter who dropped it.'

'Ah, but we have a pot. And a tank of water. And if the fire gets too large we can put it out. We've got to take a chance of some kind,' reasoned Dawlish. 'We'll start the blaze with newspapers and oddments, and then put a damp cloth on top to smoulder.'

'But Pat—supposing you do raise an alarm, what do you think will happen?' asked Felicity nervously.

'Well, either of two things. If they think the loft's on fire they'll know they've got to put it out or else get away before the house catches. If they come up we can prepare a welcome, and if they scram we can be out in two jiffs. Wouldn't be a bad idea to put those tiles back into position,' he added judicially, 'it'll stop the smoke from getting through the roof and warning 'em in the grounds. Once the alarm's raised inside the gents outside will get careless. That'll be your chance, Cedric. I'll try a frontal attack, you sneak out.'

Forbes said: 'Yes, old boy, but how do I get out when the great moment comes?'

'You break the glass at the window,' said Dawlish simply. 'You make the oven, I'll get the tiles back into position.'

'What about another little song to keep our hearts gay?' asked Forbes. 'It looks as if they'll need it.'

CHAPTER 13

A SMELL OF BURNING

Angela Boon heard their bearded captor addressed as 'Gale' with some relief. An anonymous man—quite illogically—appeared to her to be less human than a man with a name.

Gale was, in fact, trying to make up his mind what to do. Angela was alone in one room, Roger in another; which, if either, should he visit?

Another moment, and it was decided for him.

The landing guard called out suddenly:

'Gale! Quickly! They've started a fire!'

Gale spun round.

'*What!*'

He rushed up the stairs with such speed that the floor shook. The entire landing was filled with evil-smelling smoke, which was coming from the hatch doors.

'They're mad!' he gasped.

'Must be a big bonfire,' suggested the guard, 'or there wouldn't be so much smoke.' He looked at the raftered ceiling. 'Soon burn, an old place like this. Smell it?'

'Of course I smell it,' shouted Gale. He pushed the man aside and strode along the passage. 'Dawlish!'

There was silence—except for the blustering wind and the rain lashing against the windows.

'*Dawlish!*'

Another silence—and then three voices, raised in unison:

> 'Ten—little—matches
> Lying—in—a box!
> Ten—little—'

'Dawlish!' bellowed Gale, 'if you don't put that fire out you'll be burned alive, I shan't help you!'

> '. . . matches
> Lying in a box!
> If one little maa-aatch
> Should accidentally strike—'

'Dawlish!'

Silence; followed by Dawlish's voice, mildly curious.

'Is someone calling me?'

'Dawlish, you heard what I said. You'll be burned alive if you don't put that fire out.'

'But we can't,' said Dawlish. 'We're singing to keep our spirits up.'

'You'll roast alive!'

'Then I greatly fear the police will call it murder,' said Dawlish calmly, 'and hold you responsible.'

'Put that fire out!'

'But it won't be put,' protested Dawlish, 'I—'

'Pat!' That was Felicity's voice, and Gale and the man standing by him, watching the smoke creep thickly through the hatch, glanced at each other. The note in the woman's voice was very different from that in Dawlish's.

'Pat, I can't stand it. They mustn't let us stay up here, we'll—'

'Nothing we can do about it now,' said Dawlish.

'They *can't* put it out,' muttered the guard.

'Pat, stop fooling.' That was the other man in the loft, and he sounded as nervous as Mrs Dawlish. 'The place will burn like tinder.'

'Dawlish! The others are right. You'd better be serious.'

'But there's nothing I can *do*,' yelled Dawlish. 'You'll have to open the hatch!'

'If you try any tricks—' began Gale.

'Oh, have some sense!' snapped Dawlish. 'How can we try any tricks, we're—' He broke off and began to cough.

Gale said sharply: 'Put the ladder up. Christ, bring the men in from the grounds. I don't trust Dawlish, he'll make a run for it if we're not careful. Then make sure the Boon girl's locked in. Better leave one man outside,' he added, 'to watch the downstairs windows.'

'Chris' scurried off; the other began to let the ladder down.

Upstairs, Dawlish was still coughing.

No amount of ingenuity had enabled Dawlish and the others to prevent the smoke from getting into the loft, and their coughing was not altogether feigned. They heard with infinite joy Gale's order to bring the men in from the grounds, but the added order to leave one man outside, they did not hear.

While Dawlish made as much noise as possible, Forbes broke the window. He had no idea how he was to get to the ground, only a firm intention of doing so.

The ladder thumped on the floor below. Gale's orders were

being obeyed quickly, men were running. Then came the sound of the bolts being drawn back, and Felicity clutched Dawlish's hand.

Forbes laid the last piece of glass on the floor, and then put his head through the window to reconnoitre. The roof sloped steeply, but a large chimney-stack was fairly near. If he climbed out with his back towards it he could slither down and come to rest against the stack. A few wisps of smoke curled up through the window but hardly enough to attract attention.

He disappeared as the door of the hatch opened.

Pale, anxious faces peered upwards from the foot of the ladder. Gale made great play with his gun, and two others pointed their carbines toward the hatch door.

'Come on,' Gale called, impatiently.

Dawlish put his foot by the side of the smouldering heap and kicked. Rags, burning paper and a piece of wood fell out of the hole, on to the men below. One of them shouted in alarm; a shower of sparks touched Gale's head and he let out a bellow.

Felicity emptied the pot of water over him.

Dawlish jumped down.

He landed clear of the ladder. A shot rang out from the landing, and the bullet smacked against the wall close to his head. But before a second shot was fired Dawlish wrenched the automatic out of Gale's hand. The third armed man was reeling against the wall, blinded by water and smoke. Dawlish pushed Gale towards the landing guard, who fired again.

The bullet caught him in the shoulder.

Dawlish loosed a shot towards the gunman; the carbine dropped, the man clutched his arm.

'All clear, Fel,' roared Dawlish.

There followed a frantic two minutes. Dawlish grabbed Gale round the waist, and flung him bodily along the passage.

He bowled one man over. Dawlish went forward, reaching the landing in a few long strides, and before the man he had wounded could recover his wits and pick up his gun, he had grabbed the carbine and clouted him across the head.

The landing and the passage were shambles. The one uninjured man had lost all his joy of the fight, and held his hands above his head. There was an odd moment of silence. Then Felicity appeared, and calmly began to tread out the smouldering rag.

A shot rang out from the grounds.

Forbes slithered down the streaming tiles, thought for a scarifying moment that he had missed the chimney-stack, then struck it with his right foot. The guttering of the roof loomed up very close, and he grabbed at it.

The nearest pipe was two yards away, and it wouldn't be easy to crawl towards it.

The rain beat down on him until he was drenched to the skin, but he hardly noticed that. He was within a yard of the pipe now. He crawled forward again until he could touch it. Now his problem was how to lower his legs over the guttering.

It seemed an age before he was in the right position; and he knew that the chances were still against him. Gently he lowered himself over the edge. Five minutes after he had left the loft, he was hanging at arm's length from the guttering. He took one hand away; all his weight was now on one arm. He searched for the pipe with his feet, and found a joint; that helped him to ease the weight on to one leg. Next moment he gripped the pipe, but there was one thing for which he had not allowed. The pipe was slippery with the rain.

He clutched desperately. The only thing for it was to go down as fast as he could, never mind caution. He slithered down, hand over hand, hugging the pipe with his feet. Within ten feet of the ground he let go and flung himself backwards.

A shot rang out, and a bullet smacked into the wall just above him!

Crack!

A stab of pain shot through his thigh.

He got to his feet and dived towards the porch. A third shot missed him. . . .

And then, as he reached the porch, he saw Dawlish with a gun in his hand.

Crach-ack! Two shots came as one, and the man in the grounds staggered.

Before the fellow could recover Forbes was upon him, and had grabbed the gun.

It had been, according to Dawlish, a most useful morning's work. Roger fervently agreed with him.

After the furious burst of excitement everything had gone smoothly. His own share had been negligible. By the time he had forced open the window Dawlish had settled the issue. A moment or two later Dawlish had let him out, and said brusquely:

'Lend a hand in the round-up, will you?'

Roger had lent a hand with a will.

It was now known that Gale-had had five men with him; Gale himself and two of the others were wounded. One had given in.

The one uninjured man had been pressed into service in the kitchen, under Angela's supervision. Now the prisoners were in one of the bedrooms and, for security's sake, they had been bound hand and foot, and the door locked on them; as Dawlish had put it, a little peace and quiet was the order of the day. The final touch came when Forbes, who had a slight flesh wound which was now plastered comfortably, had found a crate of beer in the kitchen. Felicity and Angela had plumped for tea, while the three men decided to sample the beer.

Looking round the room, Roger reminded himself that less than an hour before their situation had seemed entirely hopeless.

He helped himself to another sandwich.

'Question is, what to do next, Pat?' asked Forbes, happily munching.

'No problem there,' said Dawlish. 'When Gale's stewed for a little longer we're going to have a chat with him. We owe him a bit for you and Angela, and Roger.'

Angela said: 'Don't take any revenge for me, *please*.'

'What a nice nature the child has,' observed Dawlish, admiringly. 'No, no vengeance, there's neither time nor excuse for it. On the other hand, Gale certainly knows a great deal that we want to find out. We'll have him in here,' he decided; 'an audience might loosen his tongue. Thinks a lot of himself, that man, and he won't want to be hurt with a gaping ring of spectators.'

'*Hurt?*' echoed Angela.

Dawlish looked at her speculatively.

'Yes, child. Hurt. Pain is a language which Gale understands, you ought to know that by now. In villainy he is only one shade less than his boss Mizzy. This affair goes much deeper than purloined pearls, you know. And you aren't the first young woman whom Mizzy has kidnapped.'

The room seemed to go cold.

'I'll be as brief as I can,' said Dawlish, 'but you and Roger both deserve an outline of the story to date. It started—or this particular stage of it started—some six weeks ago. Lord Hillmorton, of whom you've probably heard, was robbed. A large collection of precious stones was taken from his country house. But it wasn't "just another" big robbery, there was an important difference. *Very* important,' Dawlish added. 'The robbery wasn't reported to the police. Mizzy had evolved a special system. He robs, and then blackmails his victims into silence. In this case the victim's daughter was kidnapped. He was told that if he reported his loss he wouldn't see her again. Whether he was right or wrong to say nothing is neither here nor there—he decided that he couldn't risk losing his daughter. But when she wasn't returned after several weeks he couldn't stand the strain. He still didn't go to the police, but he did come to see me.'

CHAPTER 14

THE STORY

No one moved.

Angela watched Dawlish closely, her face set, her eyes bright. And Felicity Dawlish also watched her husband, as if this story were new to her as well as to Angela.

'Why should he do that?' asked Angela quietly.

'It's his reputation,' said Forbes, and paused to finish his beer. '*The* Patrick Dawlish. Secret Service and all that. *Aide* to Scotland Yard. Hang it, you've heard of the great *Dawlish.*'

'I think I have,' agreed Angela. 'Yes, I remember—Adam's spoken about him sometimes.' She smiled.

Dawlish said: 'The simple truth is that I can, and sometimes do, take chances which the police can't take. And do things which regulations prevent them from doing. Let's accept the situation as it is, shall we? Grace Hillmorton is a prisoner of Mizzy's mob, and Hillmorton asked me to try to find her. He was still anxious that the police shouldn't know what had happened. And if a man will keep silent when he's lost a daughter plus a hundred thousand poundsworth of precious stones, then he's really anxious not to talk. I gather that Mizzy spent five minutes on the telephone telling Hillmorton what would happen to his daughter if the loss of the jewels was reported before he—Mizzy—gave the all clear.'

Angela said: 'I don't quite understand why Mizzy should be so anxious, if he's got the jewels.'

'Simple,' said Dawlish. 'He wants time to dispose of them. It sometimes takes weeks to get rid of valuable gems, and it's always more difficult if they're listed by the police as stolen. It brings their value down sharply, too. I've no doubt that Mizzy sells as if he were an agent acting for Hillmorton or for others whom he persuades to keep silent over their losses. Thus he gets full market value—'

'But anyone could find out that the jewels were being sold,' protested Angela.

'Girl with all the questions,' murmured Forbes.

'She's doing all right,' said Dawlish. 'As a matter of fact, Angela, many wealthy men are selling jewels these days. But many of them don't want it to become generally known, so they sell under cover. Mizzy was quick to see the advantages of this, and jumped in with robbery-plus-blackmail.'

'I *see*,' said Angela rather doubtfully.

Roger stirred in his chair.

'Did you say there are other victims, as well as Lord Hillmorton?'

'Yes, quite a few. Mizzy will over-reach himself,' Dawlish added quietly, 'but he might do a lot of damage before he does. That's one of the reasons why I'm very glad you're free, young woman.'

'We'll have a little drink to that,' boomed Forbes. He bent down and picked up a bottle of beer.

'Where do the pearls come in, Dawlish?' Roger asked.

'Grace Hillmorton was coming away from a ball when she was kidnapped. She had the pearls then.'

'Knowing Mizzy's mob, Pat thought it possible that whoever had snatched her took the pearls without telling Mizzy,' broke in Forbes. 'In which case he might find it pretty difficult to dispose of them without Mizzy getting to know. Pat thought that if that were so, an advertisement might catch his eye.'

Roger took out his pipe and began to fill it.

'Do you still think that one of Mizzy's men took the pearls?' When Dawlish didn't answer, he went on quietly: 'The robbery took place six weeks ago, you say, and the pearls turned up on the very morning the advertisement appeared,' went on Roger. 'That's queer.'

'Not really. The advertisement has appeared every morning for nine days,' Forbes broke in.

'And will do so until further notice,' said Dawlish. 'If it were to be discontinued suddenly the police and Mizzy would think that they've been found. Whereas, they haven't.'

'They have near enough,' said Angela. 'Daddy will look after them, and—Good heavens! We haven't told him that I'm all right! Where's the telephone?'

She jumped up.

'I don't think we'll send any messages until we've had a talk with Gale,' said Dawlish quietly. 'Another hour or two won't make a lot of difference. Do you mind?'

Angela hesitated—and then gave way.

She did not yet know that her father had left the *Bay Hotel*, and obviously Dawlish had his own reasons for not wanting that news to be broken to her at this point. To cover an awkward moment Roger plunged in with another question.

'Who *is* this Mizzy?'

Dawlish said quietly: 'No one knows. And that's one of the things we might learn from Gale. Shall we have him in?'

*   *   *

Gale wasn't half the man he had been.

Before leaving him locked up Dawlish and Forbes had looked at his shoulder, and found that his wound was not serious. They had stemmed the bleeding and applied bandages, and made sure that he was in a position which would not aggravate the injury. As he came into the room they could all see that his face was pale, his beard singed, and that his collar and tie had been torn off in the scuffle.

Angela came over and sat by Roger.

'I'd really rather not stay,' she said quietly.

'Hang on for a bit,' advised Roger.

Forbes closed the door and turned the key in the lock. That was a mere piece of showmanship, because there was obviously not a chance for the man to escape with five people in the room and Dawlish standing between him and the door.

Gale shuffled forward until he was within arm's reach of Dawlish. He was a tall man, and certainly not thin; but Dawlish dwarfed him. There was something frightening in the big man's face as well as in his size. Angela slipped her hand into Roger's; he was surprised at her tension. Surely Dawlish was bluffing, in an attempt to frighten the man.

Dawlish said: 'Gale, if you want to get away without being hurt, you'll talk. How did you know where to find us?'

'We were shadowing your wife, saw her go to the estate agents in Walsham, and—'

'All right,' said Dawlish abruptly. 'How did you know we were coming here this morning?'

'Our men in Brittling saw you take this road—where else were you likely to come?'

'So one man followed my wife and another was in Brittling. Mizzy's using plenty of men, isn't he?'

'He's got plenty,' said Gale, and showed his first flash of spirit.

'You'd better be careful, Dawlish, if Mizzy gets his knife into you—'

'It's all a question of whose knife it is,' said Dawlish, 'and whom it's in. I don't like Mizzy. I hope to stop his present career. Who is he?'

Gale closed his mouth and stared defiantly.

'Who *is* Mizzy?' Dawlish asked again, and he spoke very softly. But his right hand bunched and moved slowly, as if he were going to drive his first into Gale's face.

'Who *is* Mizzy?' he repeated.

Gale remained silent.

Dawlish shot out his hand. Angela flinched. Gale dodged back, and Dawlish's hand opened before he touched the man and struck him with the palm across the cheek—a stinging but not a cruel blow. Gale's cheek was red where the blow had fallen, and he rocked a little on his heels.

'Who is Mizzy?' Dawlish asked again.

'I don't know!' snapped Gale. 'It's no use asking anyone who Mizzy is, no one knows. You needn't think—'

'Truth, friend,' said Forbes. 'The other little rats might not know who Mizzy is, but you know all right. Unclam.'

'I don't know!' Gale flared up. 'I've never seen him, I get orders from—'

He paused, and Dawlish said: 'Go on, Gale.'

'I get orders from a woman,' Gale muttered. 'Not Mizzy. When I ring him up it's always a woman who speaks to me. It's no use asking me, I don't know Mizzy.'

'But you know his telephone number,' murmured Dawlish.

The silence which followed was even more tense—and Gale set his lips as if he were determined not to speak again.

Supposing he was obstinate?

What would Dawlish do? wondered Roger.

'The number, please,' said Dawlish.

'It—it's a different one each time,' said Gale desperately, 'you don't think Mizzy would be careless, do you?'

'A flat for every day of the week, is it?' asked Dawlish. 'I doubt that, Gale, and I'm not fooling when I tell you that I'll beat you up very badly if you don't tell the truth. What number do you ring?'

'It's a different number every time,' insisted Gale. 'Not a flat, but—'

'Go *on*,' ordered Dawlish.

'A hotel! Sometimes it's the *Savoy*, or the *Berkeley*, or the *Piccadilly*, one of the big hotels. Then it's in the country sometimes; the last call I made—'

He broke off.

'You're doing nicely,' encouraged Dawlish, 'but if you keep having these pauses while you think up a new lie I shall come to the conclusion that you're making it all up. Where did you last telephone Mizzy's latest lady-friend?'

Gale said: 'You—you won't believe me. It was last night, at—'

He paused again. He was breathing heavily, and Roger thought that the man was now afraid, but not only of Dawlish. He was afraid of the consequences of his admissions. It was as if he knew that if ever Mizzy learned that he had said so much he would have little mercy on him.

'Go on,' repeated Dawlish.

'The *Bay Hotel!*' cried Gale.

At that moment Dawlish stared straight into Angela's eyes. Roger, not yet recovered from his surprise at that piece of information, moved uneasily. Why had Dawlish looked at Angela so oddly?

'I see,' said Dawlish, turning back to Gale. 'So you telephoned the *Bay Hotel*. For whom did you ask?'

'A—a Mrs Cherry.'

'*Cherry?*' echoed Forbes laughing.

'The name was Cherry!' snapped Gale, defiantly. 'I always have to use a name which has been previously decided on. After I'd finished talking to her she told me to ask for Mrs Flower next time—'

'At the *Bay Hotel*?'

'No, I shall get a message telling me where to ring,' said Gale. 'I only carry out orders and report, that's all.'

'Oh, no,' said Dawlish gently. 'You do other things. Deliver up the stolen goods, for one thing. Park the lifted ladies, for another. Do you get instructions about these from the lady or ladies with the horticultural names?'

'Yes.'

'Was Mrs Cherry old, young or middle-aged, as far as you could judge?'

'Young.'

Dawlish looked towards the window.

Roger, craning forward to see what Dawlish could see, saw a car turn into the drive.

CHAPTER 15

MIZZY?

Without saying very much, Dawlish arranged the scene quickly. Gale was taken upstairs again, Felicity and Gordon despatched to the next room, where, Dawlish said, they could see, and probably overhear, what was going on. Angela remained with him.

By that time the sound of the car's engine was very loud. Roger, looking through the window, saw that it was a large cream Packard, with a small plump man at the wheel. There were no passengers.

Forbes had secured Gale and locked him in, and was back in the hall as the bell clanged. He opened the front door, braced for guns and threats. What he saw was a little bundle of a man, with a pink face and merry blue eyes. He shook the rain off his hat, and inquired in a high, agreeable voice for Mr Dawlish.

'Dawlish?' echoed Forbes, who had been prepared to hear any inquiry but that.

'This is Valley Cottage, Valcombe, isn't it? I was given to understand—'

'Yes, he's certainly rented the cottage,' Forbes admitted, 'but we didn't know anyone else knew—rest cure,' he added meaningly.

'Rest? Cure?'

Forbes stood aside.

'Do come in. I'll see if he's up to seeing you. Shocking business, nerves.'

'Mr—Major Dawlish suffers from *nerves*?' breathed the stranger. 'Well, well! How different from what I had been led to expect!' He unloosed his muffler. 'How very distressing. But if he could see me for a minute I would be most grateful, and I feel sure that it would be good for his—ah—nerves.'

The newcomer beamed, as he followed Forbes to the sitting-room.

'Mr Dawlish—how delightful! I am really pleased to see that you are on your feet again. Your man quite alarmed me.' A plump hand was held out. 'May I introduce myself? I am Jeremiah Missingham—Mizzy to my friends.'

Only Angela, who was in a chair behind the door, showed any surprise, and the man who called himself Mizzy did not know that she was there. But Dawlish noticed Angela's reaction. She had been startled by the caller's voice, and when she saw him, as he uttered his name, a blaze of emotion—anger, horror, fear?—sprang to her eyes, then faded; but it had been too fierce a blaze for Dawlish to overlook.

'I have been most anxious to meet you,' murmured Dawlish.

'Excellent,' beamed the other, 'I felt sure my name would be familiar to you. Especially after the telephone call which I received a little while ago telling me what had happened here. My informant, I may say, was *most* impressed by your ingenuity, although—forgive me—I gathered in the course of the conversation that you owed a great deal to—ah—brute force.'

'Quite a bit,' said Dawlish.

'Ah! A man who sees himself as others see him—a rare human being, Major Dawlish, I felt sure that there would be a great deal of mutual benefit in this interview.' His eyes roamed. 'May I sit down? I—But my dear young lady!'

Angela stood up from her easy chair.

'My *dear* young lady,' bleated Missingham, 'forgive the cliché, but what a small world! Yes, indeed. How unexpectedly we meet again!' He crossed to her and held out a pink, well-padded hand which Angela did not appear to see.

'He is staying at the *Bay Hotel*,' said Angela. 'We had tea together one afternoon before my father arrived.'

'Yes, yes,' said Missingham, 'and how pleasant it was, to be sure, to meet a beautiful and cultured young lady who has also common sense—a *rara avis* these days, indeed—eh, Major Dawlish? Well, well.' He sat down in the most comfortable chair he could find. 'Well, Major Dawlish—you're surprised at my visit, eh?'

'Not remarkably so,' said Dawlish.

'Indeed! Do you know, I find that difficult to believe.'

'The forerunner of other, more profound difficulties to come, I fear,' said Dawlish smoothly. 'I will explain it to you. You were told that Gale and some of your—friends, did you say?— were having a little vacation here. Even you haven't unlimited manpower, and Gale is a very important person in the Mizzy mob, isn't he? And so I assumed that a bargainer would appear, to suggest an exchange. Lord Hillmorton's daughter, shall we say, for Gale.'

'Then you didn't expect me in *person*?'

'No, I didn't expect Mizzy in person,' agreed Dawlish.

Missingham looked at once delighted and relieved.

'Now I think I understand,' he declared. 'Very shrewd, very penetrating. Well, now—about your suggestion, Major Dawlish. I confess that Gale is a very useful man and I should find it diffi- cult to work without him. Not impossible, you understand, but it would mean that I would have to do more myself, and I do like to keep in the background. So much more comfortable. As for Lord Hillmorton's daughter . . . Well . . .' He pursed his lips and folded his hands across his stomach. 'I have a little influence with her, certainly. I think, if I were to make the request an urgent and personal one, she *might* return from her vacation and rejoin her father. Supposing I take Gale with me, and see what I can do?'

'Supposing you see what you can do, and if Grace Hillmorton returns take Gale with you,' said Dawlish.

'Ah, yes. The same suggestion from a different viewpoint, but—I will confess, Major Dawlish, that I am not convinced that you would carry out your word. You would not lie to your best friend or to a judge, but you would not regard it as a breach of your peculiar code of honour if you were to lie to me. Would you?'

'Yes,' said Dawlish.

Missingham shook his head sadly.

'I'm afraid I cannot believe that,' he deplored.

'And I find it just as hard—perhaps harder—to believe that if you took Gale away you would—er—reason with Grace Hillmorton,' said Dawlish.

'Then it's simply a question of who has the stronger hand, isn't it? One of us must take a chance; the question is—which one? Whose safety do you regard as most important? Will it hurt you to know that Grace Hillmorton will refuse to return home, as much as it will hurt me to feel that Gale will spend, possibly, a few years in jail? On the whole, I don't think that would greatly worry me, you know. It would be a nuisance, of course, but I should soon find someone to take his place. Whereas—you don't know where to find Grace Hillmorton, do you?'

'Not yet,' said Dawlish.

'My dear Major, she is a self-willed girl, and I am quite sure she will hide successfully for a very long time.'

'I didn't know she was a friend of Penelope Mayfair,' murmured Dawlish.

Missingham's hands dropped to his sides, he leaned forward, his eyes bulging. All the geniality and benevolence disappeared, to be replaced by a snarling malignance.

'*What* did you say?' he breathed. 'Has *Mayfair* told you that—'

'Mayfair sticks to the story that his wife's gone abroad,' said Dawlish, 'but I don't believe it any more than I believe that he could lay his hands on the whole of his collection.'

'I *see*,' said Missingham. 'If I thought Mayfair had talked to you—'

'He hasn't,' said Dawlish, and sprang to his feet. The movement was so swift that he reached Missingham before the man could back away. He shot out his hands and gripped Missingham by the neck, shaking him so violently that the little man's head bobbed to and fro and his teeth chattered.

The shaking seemed to go on for ever . . .

Then Dawlish flung the man back into his chair.

Only Missingham's harsh and heavy breathing broke the silence. It was several minutes before he recovered sufficiently to shake his coat into position; and now he looked at Dawlish with hatred in his eyes.

Dawlish said: 'That's just to let you know that if anything happens to Penny Mayfair you will answer for it. The same applies to Grace Hillmorton *and* the others. Don't harm them. Otherwise you will have a very rough time.'

Missingham moistened his lips.

'And if you return Grace Hillmorton I'll release Gale,' said Dawlish. 'I'll give you forty-eight hours. If you take any longer I shall turn Gale over to the police and tell them the whole story. And don't forget that the police know very little so far. If they did all those jewels you're holding until you can find the right market would drop in value overnight. You'd lose a lot of money, Missingham. Understand?'

Missingham said huskily: 'You've made yourself clearly understood, Major Dawlish.'

'That was my intention,' said Dawlish drily. 'Now get out.'

Missingham said: 'I will go—but we shall meet again.'

He went to the door, hesitated with his fingers on the handle, then changed his mind and went out. Not until he was almost out of sight did he look over his shoulder. Angela saw his expression. It was evil—menacing—malevolent. She believed that this man would gladly murder Dawlish; she could imagine unheard-of horrors being created in his mind.

Angela turned to Dawlish, and there was anguish in her eyes.

'You shouldn't have let him go,' she cried. 'You shouldn't have let him go. He'll never forgive you!'

Dawlish looked at her thoughtfully, and said a strange thing—a thing which Roger overheard as he came into the room behind Felicity.

'Aren't you *glad* I let him go, Angela?'

Angela tried to stare him out—but her eyes dropped, and she turned away.

Roger could not make head or tail of the situation, and he knew from Forbes' manner that he, too, was puzzled. Better leave the whole thing to Dawlish, he thought, and withdrew for a hot bath and the donning of clean, dry clothes. He was putting on a collar and tie when Dawlish breezed in with a cheerful smile.

'Well, Roger? Crazy gang, aren't we?'

'I've known more ordinary people,' said Roger.

'Sorry you're mixed up with us?'

The answer wasn't easy to give. But for this affair he would not have come to know Angela. And in spite of the odd incident in the sitting-room, in spite of the fact that he knew so little about her, he was in love with Angela. Yet *could he* say he was glad? That would imply being glad that she was in danger—for undoubtedly she was. And yet –

'On the whole, not sorry, eh?' said Dawlish. 'I think I can follow you. Nice girl. Mysterious family, but all the same a nice girl.'

'Mysterious?' snapped Roger. 'I don't get you.'

Dawlish laughed on a rather wry note.

'In spite of being lumped as one, a family is basically made of individuals,' he advised. 'Colonel Boon went off with the pearls; Adam and he disappeared without a word to you; Angela was— naturally—anxious to tell them she is safe and yet caved in very quickly when I asked her to postpone telling them. Doesn't all that make mystery?'

Roger growled: 'If you're suggesting that the Boons know anything about this business, you're crazy.'

'Oh, but they might,' said Dawlish. 'After all, Mizzy was staying at the *Bay Hotel*.'

'Gale probably lied to you!'

'I certainly wouldn't put that past him,' agreed Dawlish. 'On the other hand, Angela recognised Missingham. On the whole, I think we'll have to take Gale's word for it this time.'

Roger said quietly: 'Angela was kidnapped. Peter Boon is badly injured. And yet you ask me to believe that they're mixed up in it from Mizzy's side. That's nonsense!'

'Think clearly,' said Dawlish. 'I don't suggest that the Boons and Mizzy are directly associated. I think the Boons might know something about him. For instance, supposing Gale first came to Brittling to collect those pearls *from* someone. The Boons, for instance. And supposing—'

'I won't suppose such arrant nonsense!' snapped Roger angrily. 'There isn't the slightest reason for suggesting it!'

Dawlish looked calmly into Roger's eyes—and in spite of himself Roger felt his resentment evaporating. There was such confidence about this man. And at the back of his mind Roger had to admit that the Boons *had* behaved strangely—even Angela.

Dawlish said: 'Roger, don't take the Boons' integrity for granted. They may be all right. They may even be *victims* of Mizzy. Their part in this might even be wholly accidental, but—you'll be foolish to assume that it is. I'm very anxious to find out what they know, if anything, and I don't think they'll tell me. They might tell you. And you can do a useful job of trying to find out.'

'If you think I'm going to spy on them, you've made a big mistake,' said Roger heatedly.

Dawlish said gently: 'Be reasonable, old chap. You're greatly taken by Angela—and that shouldn't surprise anyone, she's the most bewitching baggage I've met for a long time. But supposing she and her family *are* crooks? Is it going to help you to live in a fool's paradise? Won't it be better if you find out the truth, even if it hurts like hell?'

Roger didn't answer.

'Whatever you find out will be confidential,' Dawlish said earnestly. 'The police need never know, unless you feel that they should. On those conditions, will you help?'

After a long pause and a great struggle with himself Roger growled:

'How can I?'

'Take Angela back to Brittling,' said Dawlish. 'Let her and the Boons string you along. I'll get in touch with you in a day or two, and if you've discovered anything you think might be useful you can let me know then. One thing in particular you might try to find out,' added Dawlish very quietly. 'Why Angela reacted so violently when she first saw Missingham, and why she lied to me by saying that she'd met him casually while they were having tea.'

'*Did* she lie?' demanded Roger.

'I'm pretty sure she did,' said Dawlish. 'Well, will you have a cut at it?'

CHAPTER 16

THE REUNION

Roger and Angela caught the bus just outside Valcoombe for Brittling.

Everyone aboard was chattering; the conductor, the long and the short distance passengers, the villagers and the townsfolk; there were only two still tongues, Roger's and Angela's.

Yet theirs was a companionable silence.

In spite of everything that Dawlish had said, Roger felt content to be with her. He did not consciously accept or reject any of Dawlish's suggestions, and was not yet troubled because he was about to set out to trick her and her family into betraying the truth. He felt no sense of disloyalty. But as they jogged along he realised that this was because he was convinced that whatever he discovered would be to the credit of the Boon family.

It was nearly four o'clock.

They had spent an hour with Dawlish, agreeing what story to tell—and it was to be a true story except in one or two details. That Angela had been taken to a cottage and kept prisoner; that Roger had been taken from Brittling by a big man whose name they had never learned; that they had all been surprised and overpowered by the gang in possession. Thereafter they were to tell the truth, omitting only the visit of Mr Missingham.

Angela had protested against these half-truths; but her protests had not carried conviction, and she had given way without serious difficulty.

Once or twice while on the bus Roger had noticed a car which followed them for a few hundred yards, then passed them, only to let them pass it a little further along. He did not recognise the man at the wheel, and he was a little apprehensive lest it were one of Mizzy's men. But Dawlish had assured him that he need fear nothing from Mizzy for a day or two—and again Roger had accepted the large man's assurance, although there was no apparent justification for it.

The bus-stop in Brittling was in the Square; and the police-station was only five minutes' walk from the terminus.

A sergeant was standing on the top step, gazing idly up and down, as Angela and Roger approached. His glance swept over them, then stiffened.

'*Is* it Mr Macclesfield?' he inquired. '*And* Miss Boon?'

'Yes,' said Roger cheerfully. 'All safe and sound.'

'Well, *this* is a fine turn-out! *Very* glad you're all right, Miss Boon, we've been worried about you—very worried indeed. Especially the Chief Inspector.'

Carfax was positively genial. He shook hands warmly, took them up to his office, and ordered tea to be sent up immediately.

'I'm anxious that my father—' began Angela.

'I'll see that he's told at once—he's at Walsham,' said Carfax. 'Apparently he was told by one of your kidnappers to go there. Cigarette, Mr Macclesfield?' He lifted the receiver, and arranged for Colonel Boon to be told and for notification to be sent to Scotland Yard and to other police forces. That done, he busied himself with the tea cups and a plate of mock cream cakes. His sourness was gone. When tea was finished, however, Sergeant Willis appeared with his notebook.

'Now—' began Carfax.

By a quarter-to-six they had come to an end.

'It's an astonishing story,' Carfax said. He smiled thinly. 'You certainly make it sound very convincing. And graphic. You say that you didn't hear this man's name? Nor the names of any of his friends?'

'No,' said Roger.

'They were very careful not to give anything away,' said Angela.

Carfax laughed on rather a high-pitched note.

'I don't think their caution will get them very far, your description of the big man identifies him pretty well,' he said. 'We shall see. I expect you are tired, Miss Boon. I'll have you driven into Walsham.'

They drove in state, sitting together in the back of a police car, to Walsham. A small market town, it boasted only one passable hotel, *The George and Dragon*. Here they found Adam Boon airing himself on the porch.

Immediately he saw Angela he hurried down the steps and pulled open the door. He helped her out, gave her a bear-like hug, then gripped Roger's hand in powerful fingers.

'Nice to see you back.'

'Where's Daddy?' demanded Angela quickly.

'He should be down any moment, but we'll go and rout him out.' He led the way up a flight of broad, carpeted stairs. 'Rooms 24 and 25. Didn't know you'd be coming, Roger, but we can fix it all right on this floor. I know there are one or two empty rooms. My father will be annoyed because we've stolen a march on him,' he added. 'Can't make out what's keeping the old boy. Can you imagine him really excited, Roger?'

'Honestly, no,' said Roger.

Adam chuckled.

'You should have seen him when he had that message from Carfax. Nearly touched the ceiling. Did Carfax tell you why we left the *Bay Hotel*?' he added to Roger. 'We thought of leaving a note for you, then decided it wouldn't be wise.' Adam looked at the numbers written in gold on the dark oak doors. 'Next but one,' he said, 'and then you'll see!'

Before they reached the door, however, another opened in the passage, and a man stepped out.

He was short and plump with a pink complexion. Glancing at them without apparent recognition, he walked past with a vague smile.

Mr Missingham reached the landing, and went downstairs without casting a glance behind him.

'What *is* all this?' demanded Adam. He stared in the wake of Mr Missingham, then looked at Angela and added sharply: 'Perfectly ordinary little chap. Arrived here a couple of hours ago. Surely you remember him, Angela?—he was at the *Bay Hotel*.'

Angela said: 'I—yes, I remember him.'

She had lost her colour, and was trembling.

'I suppose there *is* some reason for these antics,' said Adam, scowling. 'For the love of Pete, *say* something, don't stand there like a couple of supplicants at the Wailing Wall. What's come over you?'

Roger recovered first.

'We certainly didn't expect to see him,' he said, 'but we'll tell you about it later.'

Adam shrugged, and turned the handle of the door marked 24. It didn't open.

Adam pushed again.

'Odd,' he said.

Undoubtedly Roger and Angela would have been impressed by his tone but for the shock of seeing Mizzy. Even now the effect of that encounter was vivid in Roger's mind—and there was disquiet too, for why had Mizzy come to *The George and Dragon*? Could it be coincidence? Or had he come here because he had wanted to see Colonel Boon? Obviously Angela was afraid that was the explanation—and Roger remembered Dawlish's quiet assurance that she had lied about her previous acquaintance with the plump little man.

Adam rapped on the door.

There was no answer.

'Odd,' said Adam again, 'he said he'd come down as soon as he'd finished a letter he had to write.' At the same moment a porter appeared further along the passage, and Adam called out: 'Have you seen Colonel Boon, porter?'

'No, sir,' said the porter. 'Not since he was called to the telephone. Can't you get in your room, sir?'

'No, he has the key,' said Adam.

'Then I'll get a master-key—won't take a tick, sir.'

In a few moments the porter was back again.

'Ah! Here we are.' He pushed the key into the lock—but the door didn't open.

'That's queer, sir,' he said. 'Must be bolted on the inside.'

They stood in a puzzled, rather worried little group. Roger's eyes, with the keenness of perception anxiety brings, noting every intricacy in the pattern on the wall, and a tiny leaf caught incongruously in Adam's beard. Suddenly Adam drew back, then hurled himself at the door.

'No use doing that, sir, you'd need a battering-ram to get these doors down,' said the porter phlegmatically. 'What about the window?'

Adam pushed past Roger and the porter, and opened the door of Room 25. It was a large, empty room, low-ceilinged and raftered. The window was open, and before Roger and Angela could reach him he had started to climb out.

Roger said quietly: 'Don't be an ass. You'll never do it alone. Wait, and I'll give you a hand.'

Adam stood impatiently on the narrow ledge until Roger joined him.

They stood side by side, facing the wall. By linking arms Adam could put some weight on Roger. Gradually, he reached out with his right leg. Roger felt the weight fall on his arm, and Adam stretched still further, to get a footing on the next window ledge. He pushed forward inch by inch, Roger still clutching the window frame, and Angela gripping his coat.

Presently he muttered: 'I'm there. O.K.'

It was a long time, however, before he stood upright outside his father's room. He opened the window wide, thrust his head in, then drew back, casting a single, haunting glance at Roger.

By the time Angela, Roger and the porter had reached the door of Room 24, Adam had opened it.

Roger entered the room with Angela pressing close behind.

Colonel Boon lay on the floor near the bed. There was no doubt whatever that he was dead.

CHAPTER 17

SUICIDE SUGGESTED

Roger stood in front of Angela, trying to shield her from seeing her father's body and the knife lying beside him. The wound in his neck gaped, but there was no sign of a struggle.

The porter's mouth began to quiver and he ran his fingers across his forehead.

'Better—better fetch the manager,' he muttered.

Adam swung round.

'Yes, fetch him. But don't spread gossip. Understand? Don't spread gossip.'

With an ashen face Angela approached the body. If one could keep one's gaze from the terrible gash, the Colonel's face was peaceful; and very handsome. She stretched out her hand as if to touch the knife. It was small, with a bone, or ivory, handle and a narrow blade.

'I shouldn't touch anything, Angela,' Roger said gently.

Adam strode across to the dressing-table and picked up a piece of wrapping paper.

'Don't touch *any*thing,' Roger repeated. 'We'll leave that to the police.'

'I'll do what I like,' snapped Adam.

'Don't be a fool,' said Roger. 'No use losing your head. The police won't want anything touched.'

Adam turned round on him angrily. A furious tirade wouldn't have surprised Roger then; but he shrugged and swung away.

Time hung heavily; words were pointless. Roger tried to keep his mind as far as possible from the immediate tragedy.

The pearls! Colonel Boon had been killed for them! Of course.

Footsteps came along the passage. The manager entered the room, then halted on the threshold, his eyes fixed in horror on the body.

'He's—*killed* himself!'

'That's a damned lie!' snapped Adam. 'He was murdered, he wouldn't—'

'Steady, Adam,' said Roger. He turned to the manager. 'I think you should telephone the police. Chief Inspector Carfax of Brittling must be informed of this at once.'

The man nodded. He couldn't keep his gaze off the knife.

'That's a knife taken from the dining-room. I'm sure it is!' he gabbled excitedly.

'That's for the police to decide,' said Roger crisply. 'I think we should all go out,' he added, 'there's no point in staying here. We'll wait next door.'

Adam looked as if he were about to argue, but gave way. All the life and vitality had gone from Angela, and she moved towards the door obediently. They went into Room 25, while the manager, awed, excited, not yet having assimilated the possible damage likely to accrue to the hotel bookings, demanded in an unsteady voice to be put through to the police station.

The Walsham inspector was a bulky man named Peel. Businesslike and brief, he went with Roger and Adam into the next room, asked whether anything had been touched, and nodded his satisfaction when Roger told him only the window and the door, as far as he knew. Soon a sergeant and a police constable arrived, followed by a brisk little man who was introduced as Dr Pomfrey, the police-surgeon. Pomfrey examined the body, and pronounced life extinct.

By the time that was done Carfax and Willis had arrived.

Carfax, with Willis in attendance, questioned first Adam, then Roger and Angela, dealing with Angela last. This was a Carfax no longer friendly, the geniality of their last meeting laid aside.

'And you noticed nothing which might help—no suspicious person in the hotel when you arrived?' he asked Roger.

'What *is* a suspicious person?' asked Roger, irritably.

He spoke to gain time. Should he name Missingham? Keeping faith with Dawlish would not have stopped him, but he remembered Dawlish's expression when Missingham had virtually admitted holding Grace Hillmorton and Penny Mayfair prisoner. Two women in the hands of a man capable of great evil.

Carfax said: 'Did you see anyone from the cottage? The large man, for instance?'

'Good heavens, no!' Roger exclaimed. 'The only thing I noticed was a cream-coloured Packard near the gates.'

He hoped by this disclosure to render loyalty to the police and to Dawlish. He was uncomfortably aware, however, that he might have failed both.

Carfax sent a man to the yard at once, but the Packard wasn't there. Its owner, who had registered as Miller, had also gone.

He examined the knife. There were no fingerprints on it; the handle had been wiped clean. That ruled out all possibility of suicide. The knife had been in the dining-room that lunch-time. No one had noticed that it was missing.

*   *   *

The body of Colonel Boon had been removed to the mortuary. The manager had put another room at the Boons' disposal for the night, murmuring that he would have dinner sent up.

After a long silence Angela went over to the window. Her voice came to him indistinctly.

'How can we tell Peter? Peter was—' And then she broke off, and began to cry. Adam put his arms round her, in clumsy comfort. By the time a waiter arrived soft-footed, blank of face, to lay a table, the outburst had worn itself out.

Soberly they sat down to the meal, prepared to put up a calm and sensible show, yet eating very little.

Roger was still racked by doubt. Should he tell Carfax everything that had happened at the cottage?

Should he name Missingham?

He was obsessed by the knowledge of those two women in Missingham's hands—and the ever-fresh memory of Dawlish's face when the latter had said what might happen to them. He felt that a great deal might depend on his decision, and the responsibility was heavy. Halfway through the meal he decided to tell Adam the whole story, including what had been kept back from the police. It helped to talk; he could get the story in his own mind more clearly. Adam said little. One thing struck Roger as strange: his silence when Missingham's visit to the cottage was mentioned. He glanced at Angela, who was staring at her plate.

So Adam and Angela shared some knowledge of Missingham, knowledge they wanted to keep to themselves.

Adam said, rather carefully: 'This man Dawlish seems pretty sound.' He toyed with a spoon. 'I've heard of him. There's no doubt that he's *persona grata* with the police. On the other hand, how can we keep anything back from the police now? If we do, you know what they'll think.'

'That Daddy killed himself,' said Angela, 'and, *whatever* they say, I'll never believe it. He was murdered.'

Roger asked: '*Why*, Angela?'

'Damn silly thing to ask,' growled Adam. 'He had those pearls, and was murdered for them. They were worth a fortune. And they're gone.'

'What about this telephone message, and the letter he had to write?'

'Some business,' said Adam brusquely.

'Are the police satisfied with that?'

'Why the hell shouldn't they be?' demanded Adam. 'And, if it comes to that, what gives you the right to pester us with questions? Don't you believe me?'

'No,' said Roger, deliberately.

Adam pushed his chair back and started to his feet.

'That's enough from you. There was a telephone message about a business matter, and he had to write an urgent letter. That's all. And he had those pearls and was murdered for them. *That's* all.'

Roger said: 'But the matter won't rest there. Murder or suicide, whichever it was, means that all manner of questions will be asked. The police will want to know *why* he kept those pearls. They'll also want to know who kept them back when we first saw Carfax,' he added, and Adam flushed. 'I may be satisfied that it was just a piece of folly, and you had noticed the advertisement—and I daresay the police would accept that, *if* you and your father hadn't taken them from the *Bay Hotel* and brought them here. But you're going to be questioned more closely about that—Carfax and Peel have been credulous enough so far, but it's only a lead-up. That's obvious, isn't it? And you've got to decide whether to tell them the truth or make up a convincing story. We—that is, Angela and I—have to decide what to say about the bother at the cottage. And if it weren't for those kidnapped women I wouldn't hesitate for a moment. As it is, I only wish we could see Dawlish for five minutes.'

The telephone bell rang.

Roger, with a questioning look towards Adam, lifted the receiver.

'Roger Macclesfield speaking.'

'Hallo, Roger,' said Patrick Dawlish. 'How are the Boons taking it?'

'So you know.'

'Just heard,' said Dawlish. 'Poor chap. Angela's all right, I hope.'

'As far as she can be,' said Roger. 'Dawlish, we were just talking about you, and wondering whether to tell the police everything that happened, or—'

'*What?*' exclaimed Dawlish. 'Haven't you told them yet?'

'We did arrange not to,' said Roger, a little reproachfully.

'Oh, tell them the lot,' said Dawlish. 'It's too serious to keep anything back now. And for your forbearance, many thanks.'

Roger said slowly: 'Those women *are* prisoners, aren't they?'

'Oh, yes,' said Dawlish. 'But silence now won't help you or them. You'd only get yourself jailed for complicity. The police will ask you for everything you can tell them about me—don't hold your horses. And if a man from Scotland Yard turns up by the name of William Trivett, give him Felicity's love!' The familiar laughing note was in Dawlish's voice again, but it quickly faded, and Dawlish went on: 'Seriously, Roger—I'm very sorry about Colonel Boon. I know you'll help his daughter in every way you can. Anything to tell me about her, by the way? Or any of them?'

There was a sound on the telephone, as if he were being cut off. Roger spoke sharply:

'Dawlish, are you there?'

'Oh, yes, I'm here,' said Dawlish. 'But not for long. That was the police listening-in. 'Bye.'

The line went dead.

'I'm beginning to think that man's a hot air merchant,' said Adam. 'He talks far too much.'

'And I'm beginning to think that if you hadn't held those pearls back this might not have happened. It's time you realised it.'

'Roger, please—' began Angela.

Adam took a long step forward, his hands clenched, his eyes flashing furiously.

'Take that back!'

'I'll take nothing back,' said Roger evenly.

'You practically accused me of causing my father's death—take it back.'

Roger said: 'Adam, you know what's true as well as I do. The least—'

Adam let fly with a couple of violent blows. Roger put his hands up to defend himself, then struck out, and more by luck than calculation, caught the other on the chin. Snarling with rage Adam literally sprang at him.

'Adam!' cried Angela. 'Adam!'

The door opened and Carfax and another man appeared on the threshold. Carfax jumped forward, caught Adam by the shoulders, and spun him round.

The newcomer—tall, dark, good-looking—glanced from him to Roger, then demanded sharply;

'What's all this about?'

'Who—who are you?' gasped Roger.

'This is Superintendent William Trivett, of New Scotland Yard,' said Carfax.

CHAPTER 18

TWO MEN SHAKE HANDS

If a man from Scotland Yard turns up, by the name of William Trivett, give him Felicity's love, Dawlish had said, and here was Trivett—authoritative, capable, obviously twice the man Carfax was—a man who wouldn't be put off by evasions, or easily deceived by lies.

'Well, what's it all about?' he demanded again.

Angela put her hands to her lips—a plea for silence; that was understandable. She would not want it known that Adam had kept the pearls back; everything else could be told without discredit to any living Boon, but not that. And Roger flickered his right eyelid understanding, and answered the Yard man coolly.

'We had a difference of opinion.'

Trivett swung round on Angela.

'You're Miss Boon, I understand. What's the meaning of this quarrel? Hasn't your brother *any* sense of decency? Come on—I want to know all about it.'

Roger said doggedly: 'It was a private quarrel, of no interest to the police.'

Trivett said coldly: 'Let me warn you, Mr Macclesfield, that you are already in an extremely difficult position. I don't know what Dawlish told you at the cottage, but if you think he can smooth over any difficulties you get in with the authorities you are in for a big surprise. You'd better come with us,' he added, and half-turned on his heel. 'You can get patched up at the police-station. Maybe you'll be safer there,' he added, with a meaning glance at Adam.

Angela said: 'You've no right to arrest him!'

'No?' asked Trivett. 'I think you'll find that there are plenty of charges we could prefer against him. But he hasn't been charged yet. I'm asking him to come along to the police-station and make a statement.'

'Roger, don't go!' exclaimed Angela. 'Don't let them take you away, they've no right to, you needn't go. Adam! He needn't go with the police, need he?'

Trivett broke in: 'Miss Boon, I shall probably want you to come to the station with me later on. Macclesfield, you can please yourself whether you come willingly to make another state-ment—a complete one this time—or whether you come under charge. And I don't intend to waste time,' he added abruptly. 'Too much time has been wasted in this affair already. I suppose you're aware,' he added coolly, 'that if the truth had been told immediately you reached Brittling this murder *might* have been avoided.'

Roger said quickly: 'Then it *was* murder?'

Trivett's mouth shut tightly. Obviously he had said more than he had intended.

'Are you coming with me, Macclesfield?'

Roger said: 'Oh, all right. Angela, don't worry—Dawlish agrees that we ought to tell them everything. In any case, I expect they know a great deal by now; they're expert listeners-in.'

* * *

Being questioned by Superintendent Trivett was an ordeal. He questioned coldly, made points which most certainly would not have occurred to Carfax, and maintained the pressure for nearly an hour, although Roger, in his revised statement, had told the whole truth—except about Adam taking the pearls.

He felt limp and anxious when the questions were over. Although his knowledge of criminal law was vague, he thought it possible that he had committed offences enough to be held in the police cell overnight, and charged next morning. He dreaded the thought of Angela being left alone with Adam at *The George and Dragon*. Adam had gone to pieces; he would be no sort of companion for Angela on such a night as this.

They had talked in Carfax's office, and at the end of it Carfax and Trivett left the room together. Now that he was alone—and for the first time since the Colonel's body had been found—Roger could think about this tragic development and its significance. Murder, cold-blooded and cruel, had been committed once; and might be done again. There was danger for Angela because she was Boon's daughter. Adam's manner was strange; it might well be the result of a guilty conscience, for there was no doubt that the Boons were more deeply involved than Roger had at first believed.

How much did the police know?

Could they charge Angela with any crime?

The door opened and Carfax appeared, holding a long, typewritten statement. He put it into Roger's hand.

'Read that, please, and sign if you agree that it's a true record of what you have just told the Superintendent and me.'

Roger looked down the statement quickly. Though there were a few words in it which he hadn't used, there was nothing to which he could take exception.

Carfax witnessed the signature, and then told him he could go. No-one accompanied him from the office. He felt chilled; the police were suspicious, even hostile. Although he could see no one, he felt sure that every step he took would be watched. He made his way quickly to *The George and Dragon*. Entering by a side door he leapt up the stairs and tapped sharply on the door of Number 25.

Adam looked up with an eager, hopeful expression which disappeared the moment he saw Roger.

'I thought it was Angela,' he said.

'Have the police taken her for questioning?'

'Yes, damn them!' Adam ground out a half-finished cigarette in an ash-tray, and then said a little awkwardly: 'About that dust-up, Roger. 'Fraid I lost my head. My fault, my fault entirely.'

He held out a hand.

The gesture was unexpected, especially from Adam.

'Now let's forget it,' he went on. 'One thing's obvious, we must all pull together. Peculiar show, isn't it? If the police only knew it, they ought to question me, as I more or less started the whole business. You were quite right about that.'

'We're all to blame,' said Roger generously.

Adam turned to him.

'Roger—give me a straight answer, will you? Do you think I ought to tell this Trivett man that I actually took the pearls out of your pocket?'

'I really don't see how it would help,' said Roger quietly. 'You'd only make things worse for yourself. The police know that one of us took them—or, rather, kept them from Carfax—and it doesn't make much difference who it was, especially as they guess we were all party to it. I hope to heaven they don't pick on Angela and make her break down,' he added harshly. 'I think I'll go along to the police-station and—'

'Don't you worry too much about Angela,' said Adam with a

wry smile. 'Leave the police to do that. She can be the clammiest clam you ever met.' He moved restlessly. 'This place stifles me! I'd like to walk for miles. I suppose the police would clap me in jug if I dared to attempt it.'

'I don't see how they could,' said Roger practically. 'No reason why you shouldn't go for a walk, if you want to. I'll stay until there's some news of Angela.'

Adam opened the door, and Roger walked with him down the stairs.

As they reached the steps they saw Angela and a young, very attractive woman walking towards the hotel.

Roger's heart leapt.

He waved, and Angela waved back.

'But it's Ruth!' cried Adam joyously.

He bounded down the steps, and all but hugged Angela's companion. Linking arms with both women he returned to *The George and Dragon*, his face alight with satisfaction.

Roger met them at the foot of the steps.

Casually, the newcomer was introduced as Ruth Marraday, an old friend.

It appeared to Roger that she could be more than that.

Dark, exceedingly attractive, once settled in Room 25 she turned impulsively to Adam.

'Adam, I'm so terribly sorry.' She gripped his hand.

He *had* forgotten; but now the weight of unhappiness seemed to drop on him like a heavy blanket. He scowled, he became moody and sullen. Ruth accepted this as if she had known what to expect. It was Roger who offered Ruth a drink, and poured out a stiff whisky and soda for Adam.

Adam pushed it away.

'I don't want it. How airless the place is! Ruth, come for a walk, will you?'

'Yes, darling, if you like.'

'It's nearly dark,' Angela protested. 'Don't go far.'

'All the more chance of losing those confounded police,' growled Adam. 'Come on, then.'

Ruth shot an understanding glance at Angela before they went out. Angela brushed her hand across her forehead and turned away—to hide tears, thought Roger.

Slowly, she turned round.

'Oh, Roger!'

And then she was in his arms, pressing against him, and he could hear her heart beating, feel her warm cheek against his. They stood like that for a long time, while the sobs shaking her gradually lessened.

He led her to a chair, kneeling beside her.

Angela said in a muffled voice: 'How comforting you are. And how I need comfort, Roger!'

'I'll do anything—*anything* I can to help,' murmured Roger huskily. 'I know it's not the time or place to say what I'm going to say, but I can't help it. Angela, I love you. From the first moment I saw you, I—I began to fall hopelessly, desperately, in love with you. And now nothing you say, nothing that might happen, can alter it.'

She didn't answer, and he felt her stillness like a reproof.

He said stiffly: 'I'm sorry, Angela. I'm acting like a brute. Forget it.'

'Oh, Roger!' she cried.

Half-laughing, half-crying, she kissed him.

'I know what you're thinking,' said Angela in a small, breathless voice, 'and you mustn't, darling. It isn't wrong to talk of being in love just because of what's happened, and I know that he liked you. I suppose we would have gone on for months, feeling the same but without having the courage to say so, if it hadn't been for this, and so—and so *some* good has come out of it.'

'And Adam will be delighted,' went on Angela, her voice a little higher. 'He was terribly upset after you'd gone off with the police. Have you—have you made it up?'

'Of course!'

'I don't know about "of course",' said Angela. 'He was really insufferable.' She paused, and then added abruptly: 'He's taken this—this tragedy very hard. I hope that he *will* marry Ruth. He's—hard to please, you know; I doubt if any man in England has had so many lovely women in love with him. But he's more serious with Ruth than with any of them, and I know she's very much in love with him. That's why she's here. She read in the papers that Peter had been hurt and what had happened to me, and she came at once. Perhaps this will make up Adam's mind for him. Good out of evil. It *is* true.'

'Of course it's true,' said Roger. He put his arm round her. 'You know, darling,' he said unsteadily, 'I find it very difficult to come back to earth. For a start, tell me how you got on with the police.'

'Rather well, I think. I quite liked him—what's his name? Something that reminded me of hedges. I didn't give anything away about Adam being the one who kept the pearls back, but I told them everything else, except where the cottage is. I—Roger! That was right, wasn't it?'

'Perfectly all right,' Roger assured her.

'Thank heavens for that.'

Roger said: 'There's one thing I ought to say—'

'You've said *everything*,' said Angela eagerly. 'Everything that matters. Don't spoil it, Roger—you look terribly serious, almost as if you're going to make a confession.'

Roger forced a laugh.

'Hardly that,' he said. 'Darling—'

He stopped; it wasn't easy to break the spell which had fallen upon them, but—it had to be done.

'No confession,' he promised. 'Angela, how well did your father know Missingham?'

She went still, her hands gripped tightly, her eyes solemn. He wished the light were better, because he could not see her expression properly.

The silence dragged on.

Then Angela said: 'Roger, he *didn't* know Missingham.

'Oh,' said Roger.

So she could lie to him.

The brightness, already dimmed, went out of his mind. Where he had felt exhilaration and wonder he now felt a great weight of depression.

CHAPTER 19

VOICE IN THE NIGHT

'Roger,' said Angela. 'Roger, please.' She jumped up and crossed the room quickly. He could see her reflection, in a wall mirror. Two Angelas; the Angela who said she was in love with him, and the Angela who had lied about her father and Missingham. 'Roger, he's dead,' she said. 'There's no need for anything to come out now. And it's much better for you to know nothing. I—*I* know little enough,' she went on earnestly. 'I've never probed, I didn't want to know too much, and—it's better for you to know nothing.'

Roger said: 'If I don't know everything, how can I help you?' He moved towards her. 'It's too late for entire ignorance, and partial ignorance is dangerous. I already know that you knew Missingham, that he frightened you.'

'Oh,' said Angela.

She put her hand to her hair, and began to twist a few strands round her fingers. He wanted to stride across the room and take her in his arms—but he made himself stand where he was.

She said in a small voice: 'Did Dawlish tell you?'

'Yes. He noticed the way you behaved when Missingham came into the room at the cottage, and told me of it.'

'I was afraid he might do that.'

Roger said gruffly: 'He suggested that you and your family might—might know Missingham and the Mizzy mob. He asked me to find out, and I promised I would.' She didn't speak, so he went on: 'And there are those other missing women. You know about them. If there's anything we can say or do to help we must try.'

Angela said quietly: 'Two unknown women. Yes, that has an appeal it would be useless to fight. Well, this is all I can tell you. I knew that Daddy was in serious trouble. I didn't know what it was about. He, Adam and Peter, made a conspiracy of it, and I was told nothing at all. They sent me down here ahead of them, because they said they had some urgent business which would take them away from home for ten days, and that I needed a holiday more than they. It all seemed rather childish to me, except the face that Daddy was really frightened of something— or someone. And I think it was Missingham. I heard them quarrel once; a terrible quarrel. I assumed that Missingham was blackmailing him, and when I saw Missingham at the *Bay Hotel* it nearly bowled me over—as it did at the cottage.'

'Yes,' said Roger when she paused, 'it would do.'

'You see, it isn't as if I know *why* Missingham was black-mailing him,' said Angela. 'One imagines such terrible things. That's why I felt, and still feel, so helpless. I'm not keeping it back, I just don't *know*.'

Roger gripped her hands tightly.

'And that's why I was so terrified that—that he'd killed himself,' said Angela. 'The police did say it was murder, didn't they?'

'Yes, they said so,' said Roger, 'and Trivett wouldn't have said that unless he were pretty sure.'

'It's bad enough to think that he was murdered, but it would be ten times worse to think that he'd killed himself,' said Angela.

'I don't know whether he was killed for those pearls or why it was—and, Roger. I don't really *want* to know. I'm frightened of what might come out. Don't try to find out, Roger, just let things take their course.'

Roger lay in bed thinking of all that Angela had said.

Soon after she had finished Adam and Ruth had returned, flushed and warm from a long walk. They had talked freely enough about the general situation, but not about anything which concerned Missingham, and no one had ventured any theories about the Colonel's death; it was as if Adam and Ruth had conspired to say as little as possible about it.

Ruth was staying at *The George and Dragon*.

They had used Room 25 as a kind of common-room, and it had been half-past twelve before they had all left for their own apartments.

Roger had been in bed an hour, and was still wide awake.

He could understand what Angela felt, but—was she right to carry on as she was doing? Any man who could kidnap women, holding them to ransom, threatening their lives, had a terrible capacity for evil, and—he must be stopped.

Information which Adam and Peter might be able to give the police could well lead to his capture.

And if they wouldn't tell the police, would they tell Dawlish? Supposing he were to say firmly that either they must tell the police at once, or he would tell Dawlish. Curious how much faith he had in Dawlish, how relieved he would be when Dawlish knew.

The more he pondered, the more certain he was that Adam would oppose such a course; but then, Adam would oppose anything which ran counter to his own ideas and decisions. Angela? He believed that she would understand, and agree.

Angela . . .

Sleep hovered near; he forgot the issues of the morrow and thought of that precious hour when they had been alone, and when they had talked of the things which were so close and dear to them. Dreams? Yes, they were dreams, and later when he came to think seriously about them he would have to face the practical difficulties, but—why not dream for a little while?

He went to sleep.

Detective-Sergeant Willis was tired, yet it would be four hours before relief came. He did not resent the spell of night duty; he was even pleased that he had been selected, because the man from Scotland Yard had been so emphatic on the need for a reliable man, but—one couldn't help feeling tired. He'd had a long day.

He sat in an armchair in an alcove near the landing. He could see Macclesfield's door in a mirror which had been carefully placed so that it reflected the whole length of the passage. That had been Trivett's suggestion, because it enabled Willis to keep out of sight while seeing all that went on. It had been a bit tricky early on, because that friend of Boon's, a woman named Marraday, had gone up to her room, and Boon had seen her to her door. Only to her door, Willis noted with approval; he had come down again almost immediately.

It was now two o'clock, time he took a turn along the passage. The carpet would deaden the sound of his footsteps. And if there were the slightest movement at any door, or on the stairs, he would know in a flash.

He stood up and looked cautiously over the top of the screen. Dark, empty passage, empty staircase, empty landing; and a faint smell of beer and spirits.

Ah, it was good to stretch his legs.

Every door was locked. A snoring sound came from Boon's room and Willis grinned. A man who snored always gave him a fellow-feeling; he himself snored, and his wife didn't let him forget it. But wouldn't he like to be in bed now!

He turned back towards the screen.

Within a yard of it a fresh sound reached his ears, and he turned sharply. As he did so, a cloth was dropped over his face. A hand moving very rapidly pushed a gag into his mouth.

'Quietly, quietly,' murmured Forbes. 'Don't want to hurt you.' He forced Willis to a chair, and with quick adroit fingers tied him to it.

Roger slept dreamlessly once he had dropped off. He knew nothing of what had happened on the landing, and he did not hear the faint creak as the door of his bedroom opened.

Through the mists of sleep he heard and felt something; a hand; a voice. He started, and his eyes flickered open.

'Steady,' breathed the voice. 'No cause for alarms and excursions. You *are* Roger, aren't you?'

It was dark, but the voice was familiar.

'Shock over?' asked Forbes. 'Okay—don't make too much noise, old chap, I've already earned twelve months for assaulting a policeman; if they get me for burglary too I'll have a dose of penal servitude.'

'What the devil are you doing here?' demanded Roger.

'I come as an emissary of Patrick's. What else would drag me here in the dead of night,' said Forbes piously. 'I understand the matter is urgent,' he went on. 'Patrick thinks that things are going to speed up now that murder's been done. And he isn't at all sure that the man who called himself Mizzy will honour his agreement to exchange Gale for Grace Hillmorton— you *do* remember, don't you?'

'Of course I remember, but—'

'And that makes your part more important than ever,' went on Cedric. 'Dawlish can't telephone you about it as the police are watching the switchboard. Any news from the Boon family yet?'

Roger didn't answer.

'Come, chum,' urged Forbes. 'No fooling, it's a matter of life and death. There are four policemen watching this pub, and I've taken a chance by getting through the cordon—it'll be twice as difficult to get out. We think it's as important as that.'

The reasoning was convincing. Roger had decided to tell the police or Dawlish—but he'd meant to wait until morning, and so deliver his ultimatum to the Boons. If he were to talk now, then the thing would be done, and Adam and Angela would not be able to bring pressure to bear to dissuade him. Probably it was better this way.

'There is something,' he said slowly. 'Angela thinks her father was being blackmailed. There was a quarrel between him and Missingham.'

'When?'

'I don't know—fairly recently, I gather. The brothers know all about it, but Angela says she doesn't. And I believe her.'

'My dear chap, of course you do,' said Forbes. 'Next item, who's the dark-haired beauty who arrived from the police-station with Angela tonight?'

'Ruth Marraday. She's a friend of Adam's—rather more than a friend according to Angela.'

'Thanks. Now, will you tell me as quickly as you can what happened when you got here, how Boon was killed, exactly how Adam and Angela reacted?'

Roger began to talk. He was glad to be able to tell the story to Dawlish's friend. Sleep was far away, and he remembered most of the details. And Forbes listened intently. Someone walked briskly along the street outside, the sound of the footsteps came clearly into the room.

Roger said: 'And that's the lot, as far as I can remember.'

'Sure there's nothing else?'

'Nothing of importance.'

'Good. Now for instructions. Stay here. Sit on any bright notions which the remaining Boons might have for solving the problem. Don't tell the police where the cottage is. Dig out more of this family bother with Mr Missingham, if you can, and be prepared to hear from us when you least expect it.'

'Right.'

Forbes gave a ghost of a chuckle.

'Now, I wonder if I'd better leave by the door, or try the window? Not much of a drop, is it, and I've had plenty of experience lately. I—'

He broke off with an exclamation of alarm—for a bright beam of light shone from the window, full on his face.

CHAPTER 20

FORBES FALLS

Forbes snatched up a pillow and flung it at the torch. The beam of light wavered, slashed across the ceiling, and then pointed towards the floor. A man gasped—and they saw a hand waving wildly. Forbes streaked across to the window, and leaned out.

'Hold tight, I've got you!'

Roger flung back the bedclothes and leapt to his assistance. Forbes was holding on to the wrist of a man who would otherwise have fallen.

Roger took the man's wrist, and held his weight. Forbes climbed out of the window, and, clutching the creeper, went down hand over fist.

There was the sound of creeper torn from the wall, and the thump of Forbes landing. He must have fallen hard, Roger thought. The click of a door shutting partially reassured him, and he turned his full attention on the dangling policeman. The man weighed a ton.

Sweat stood on Roger's forehead.

'Get a grip with your feet,' he muttered, 'I can't hold you much longer.'

All the man's strength seemed to have gone into his lungs, for he began to shout:

'Stop him—police! Help! Stop him, stop him!'

'You'll fall!' Roger cried. 'Keep still!'

The policeman came to his senses at last, and found a foothold. Lights came on. Adam called out.

'What's up?'

Too exhausted to answer, Roger heaved the policeman's body over the window sill.

By trying to turn success into a triumph, the Walsham policeman had achieved failure. He had heard voices in Roger's room, and had managed to climb up to the window. All this he told to Trivett and Carfax, who arrived half-an-hour after Forbes had escaped.

Roger faced the man from Scotland Yard, and realised that this was going to be his most difficult interview.

They were in Roger's bedroom.

Adam had been among the first to arrive on the scene, but neither Angela nor Ruth Marraday had been disturbed. Although Carfax had obviously been on edge to ask questions, Trivett had not yet put a single query to Roger.

Should he name Forbes? If he did this, Forbes would almost certainly be charged with the attack on Willis—and Carfax had made it clear that it was a serious offence. So would his be if he withheld information! He could lie, but if the police caught him out, he would almost certainly be lodged in a police cell. Had he only himself to think about he might take a chance, but there was always Angela.

The telephone-bell rang.

Trivett lifted the receiver.

'Superintendent Trivett—' His voice changed, grew sharper. 'No, you can*not* speak to Mr Macclesfield,' he said.

Roger was sure that Dawlish was on the line.

After a pause, Trivett said emphatically: 'No!'

'Who is it?' demanded Carfax in an undertone. 'If it's that man Dawlish—'

Trivett said: 'Hold on a minute.' He covered the mouthpiece of the receiver and turned to Carfax. 'Check the call, will you,' he whispered urgently, 'it *is* Dawlish.'

Carfax bounded from the room, and Trivett gave a half-grin as he uncovered the mouthpiece of the receiver. 'All right, Pat. Hold on. Macclesfield—' He beckoned Roger.

Roger grabbed the telephone.

'Hallo, Dawlish!'

'Hallo, Roger,' said the big man in his half-laughing voice. 'Excitements, I hear. Tell the police that it was Cedric—if you don't they might think it was me,' he added, and laughed. 'Just carry on, you're doing fine.'

He rang off. There was silence, while Adam looked speculatively at the Scotland Yard man, and Roger showed his astonishment. Trivett was smiling as if to himself.

He said: 'Patrick Dawlish is a remarkable man. I can risk giving him more latitude than Carfax dare do.'

'Well, well!' exclaimed Adam. 'When I commit a crime I hope you'll come after me.'

'Maybe I *am* after you,' said Trivett cryptically.

Adam laughed . . .

Carfax hurried in.

'It was from an A.A. box a mile outside the town,' he said importantly. 'We'll get him this time, that Mercedes-Benz can't get away again.'

Dawlish left the A.A. box and stepped into a Morris 10. Felicity was at the wheel. The headlights spread over the hedgerows and glinted on the wires as she eased off the brakes. Soon they were driving towards Walsham. They did not speak until Felicity had turned off the main road and into a field. The car bumped over the rutted cart-track at the entrance, and then over uneven meadowland. She pulled up behind a haystack.

'We're not going to sleep *here*,' she said spiritedly.

'Too true we're not,' agreed Dawlish. 'Nor are we going to stay near Walsham a minute longer than we must, either, I feel too conspicuous. Pity Cedric injured his ankle.'

'He's being well looked after,' said Felicity.

'*Ye Olde Tea Shoppe*,' mused Dawlish. 'Yes, undoubtedly he fell on his feet there all right, injured ankle and all. Wonderful way he has with middle-aged women, isn't it? However, he's not our main worry.' He lit the cigarette. 'Bill Trivett was helpful, bless his heart, but Carfax will be spiteful if he gets half a chance.'

'Is it worth antagonising him?' demanded Felicity.

'Oh, yes,' said Dawlish confidently, 'well worth it.' He rested a hand on his wife's shoulder. 'Must be able to keep in touch with the remaining Boons. They know much, much more than anyone else outside Mizzy's immediate circle. Probably even Angela, although Roger doesn't want to believe it.'

'Not so fast,' said Felicity. 'Do you still think that Missingham and Mizzy are two different people?'

Dawlish chuckled.

'I do, my sweet—and there's something I haven't told you yet. Confidential report on Mr Jeremiah Missingham, from a London agency. Missingham, under the name of Morris, was on the stage for a long time. But Mizzy doesn't act, he's the real bad lot. Oh, there's a man who calls himself Mizzy, no doubt of that—and the question of his identity is a major one.'

'No ideas?' asked Felicity quietly.

Dawlish said: 'Plenty, but too vague as yet to air. My need at the moment is to shanghai a Boon. We can't very well snatch Adam or Angela, they're being watched too closely. Hallo, here are the police.'

He leaned forward as car headlights swept the main road a hundred yards away. A small kiosk, the A.A. box, showed up plainly. The car stopped beside it. Two men jumped out.

Dawlish chuckled.

'They're probably going over it for fingerprints,' he said. 'And they're after the *Mercedes*, which should be in Northumberland by now. Darling—how do you suggest we get a Boon?'

'I suggest you don't,' said Felicity. She turned to Dawlish. 'Pat, tell me, are you playing fair? You convinced me at the start that by acting on your own you were more likely to get Penny Mayfair and Grace Hillmorton free—but is that true now? The police know so much. Mizzy will almost certainly realise how much they know, and—' She broke off.

'Act accordingly,' murmured Dawlish.

'Well, won't he?'

Dawlish said quietly: 'Darling, Mizzy will try to bargain or otherwise deal with us before this show's over. He stands to lose too much if the police catch him. So I propose to keep away from the police as much as possible, and to set a trap for Mizzy in person. And the more I know about him, the stronger my hand when it comes to a showdown.'

After a long pause, Felicity said: 'I suppose you're right. We've gone too far to draw back at this stage, but now Cedric's laid up you can't do everything yourself.'

Dawlish said encouragingly: 'Tim and Ted will come from London if we give them a ring in the morning, and they'll bring the crowd. Bill Farningham *might* be particularly helpful in this case, he knowing all about hospitals.'

He broke off, and laughed.

After a pause, Felicity laughed with him.

Peter Boon lay in the small private ward at the Brittling Hospital.

It was half-past three—visiting hours. He could hear voices from a nearby general ward, and everywhere there was the patter of footsteps.

He was extremely worried. In the middle of the morning he had received two visitors: Carfax and Superintendent Trivett of New Scotland Yard.

Trivett had told him about his father.

Afterwards, when the detectives had gone, he realised that they had told him themselves in the hope that he would say something which might help them—he knew now that they suspected his father of some kind of complicity in the affairs of the man called Mizzy.

Trivett had assured him that Angela and Adam would be allowed to see him that day.

He had expected them before this. If they didn't come, surely it meant that the police had prevented them and, for some reason, were holding them prisoner.

Until the visit that morning a policeman had been in the ward with him all the time, but since then he had been left completely on his own.

A clock struck a quarter-to-four.

'I can't stand this waiting,' he muttered, 'I must see Angela!'

He pushed back the bedclothes and would have been out but for a tap at the door.

'Who's that?'

A gruff, unfamiliar voice answered him.

'May I come in?'

Without waiting for an answer, the speaker opened the door

and stepped inside. There were two men, both of them big and powerful. They closed the door, and one of them stood at the foot of the bed while the other went to the window. This was a ground-floor room, and he could see the red brick wall of another wing of the hospital across a bare courtyard.

'Well, what's this about?' demanded Peter.

The man at the foot of the bed said: 'You've heard of Patrick Dawlish, haven't you?'

'Dawlish? Vaguely,' said Peter.

The man grinned disarmingly.

'Such is fame. The fact is, he's the chap whose helping your sister and brother. At the moment the police are rather rattled about them.'

Peter cried: 'Then they're crazy! I—Look here, where are they? Have the police arrested them?' He could hardly get the words out quickly enough.

'Not yet, but there's no telling what fool tricks the police will get up to, is there? Boon, I don't know what this is all about, but I do know your sister wants to see you, and the police won't allow you to meet. I think a meeting could be arranged, if you'll take a chance.'

'Just try me,' said Peter eagerly.

'Right! Where are your clothes?'

Peter scowled.

'They've taken them away. I'd have been out of here before now if I had a pair of trousers!'

'We've arranged for that.' One of the men produced an inconspicuously packed bundle of clothes, and the other, a pair of plimsolls.

The man by the window said: 'Shall we go out by the window or take a chance and go through the hospital?'

'Window,' said the hefty man firmly.

* * *

They were not stopped as they drove through Brittling. Those people who stared at the *Lagonda* were luxury-model worshippers, and had no interest in its occupants. Peter leaned against a pillow, which had been thoughtfully provided, and wished he could think straight; but his head was whirling.

He dozed . . .

'You know, Ted,' said one of the men, 'I don't quite get it. Pat said there would almost certainly be a policeman in the ward, and we'd have to take a chance with him, and Pat isn't often wrong.'

'Shouldn't worry too much, Tim,' said Ted. 'Local police have their moods, you know. Probably shorthanded with traffic, and decided that Boon could be left to the hospital staff for the rest of the day.'

'But the staff wasn't taking much interest in him,' protested Tim. 'I don't know that I like it.'

Ted turned and looked at him, for they were driving along a straight stretch of road and there was no oncoming traffic. His ugly face was wrinkled with perplexity.

'I don't quite get you,' he said.

'I'm wondering if this is a deep-laid scheme,' explained Tim. 'Just like Bill Trivett to let us get away with Boon and then follow us, so that he can put his hands on Pat. If he has—'

'It presupposes that Trivett guessed Pat would try to get Boon out of the hospital,' objected Ted.

'And Trivett's capable of guessing,' Tim said warmly. 'If that's what's happening, Trivett won't have us followed by an ordinary police-car, he'd know we'd twig, he'd have us followed by a car we wouldn't suspect.' Tim looked over his shoulder. The only car behind them was a shooting-brake, on which the sun shone brightly. 'That's been on our tail since we left the High Street,' he declared firmly. 'Can you shake it off?'

'Try me,' said Ted, and trod heavily on the accelerator.

A disappointed police-sergeant reported to Trivett and Carfax early that evening. He had followed the Lagonda seven miles out of Brittling, and then it had shown him a clean pair of wheels. His 'van' could do eighty-five, but the *Lagonda* had walked away from him. He had radioed a warning and given a description of the *Lagonda*, and then turned back.

'And the *Lagonda* hasn't been reported!' snapped Carfax.

Trivett said thoughtfully: 'Dawlish has a hideout somewhere near, that's the answer. I hoped we'd find it this way, but—' He broke off with a shrug.

'I can't see any reason for taking it so lightly,' said Carfax tartly. 'This man Dawlish appears to me to be extremely dangerous.'

'Dangerous? Yes, in some ways,' agreed Trivett. 'Mizzy probably isn't feeling very secure at the moment. But Dawlish is taking chances. Playing the fool by assaulting a policeman when he knows that it is more than likely to be brought home to him isn't like Dawlish. He must feel sure that he can get results which for some reason or other we can't. If you knew Dawlish—'

'I know enough about him to see that he's a damned nuisance,' snapped Carfax waspishly. 'You take the matter of assaulting one of my men *very* lightly. I must protest, Superintendent, and in compliance with my duty shall be compelled to report to the Chief Constable that I do not approve of your attitude.'

'Certainly,' Trivett said mildly, 'if you feel that way. Of course, your Chief Constable may ask you whether you can show any instance where I've neglected a chance to catch Dawlish. He might even wonder whether Dawlish's man would have escaped from *The George and Dragon* if any other man had been at the window. If it comes to that,' added Trivett, his voice sharpening, 'I doubt whether a Flying Squad car would have lost that *Lagonda*. I'm not complaining, Carfax, but if you're going to report on the failure to catch Dawlish we'll produce all the facts.'

Carfax flushed.

'Meanwhile, we might save time by getting on with the job,' said Trivett. 'Dawlish thinks that Peter Boon can give useful information—that's what I suggested when I advised leaving Boon unwatched for a few hours. We might have another go at Adam Boon.'

'*I* think we'll get more results from Macclesfield,' said Carfax, his voice glacial. 'You'll never convince me that that man and the Boons were complete strangers when they first went to Brittling. *Never.*'

'All right, we'll try him,' said Trivett, 'but you might remember this, Carfax. The Mizzy mob is one of the most powerful and dangerous in England. Its leader is ruthless and unscrupulous, and we've been trying to find him for far too long. We've always known that he worked differently from most crooks, and, thanks to Dawlish, we now know one of his methods of working. And it's quite true that Lord Hillmorton's daughter and the wife of Captain Mayfair have been away from their homes for a period of from eight weeks to three months. I've had a report on that from the Yard, and I've asked for another report and photographs of the two women. The second report might reveal a situation more serious than we've yet suspected—and explain why Dawlish is behaving as he is.'

'I strongly disapprove of Dawlish's methods,' barked Carfax.

'There are times when I'm more interested in results than how they're achieved,' said Trivett.

'Obviously we are not likely to reach agreement on that,' said Carfax coldly. 'Shall we see Macclesfield now?'

As they climbed out of the car before *The George and Dragon* a van drew up in front of them. The driver opened the back doors of the van, and lugged out a large wicker hamper. He was a small, wiry man, with a grimy face and very long hair, and Trivett looked at him curiously. Carfax stalked towards the entrance and disappeared.

The porter grumbled as he helped the driver with the hamper. He looked at the label.

'Carfax? Why, that must be *Inspector* Carfax, but he doesn't live here.'

'It's addressed here, ain't it?' demanded the van driver.

'I can't sign for Inspector Carfax,' protested the porter. 'I'll get him.'

'I'll sign for it,' said Trivett, moving forward.

He signed a dirty scrap of paper, headed: *Brittling District Carriers*, and the man nodded and went off. Carfax came back into the hall, having been summoned by the porter, and looked at the hamper in surprise and with disapproval.

'Better open it up,' Trivett suggested formally, 'especially if you're not expecting it.'

'I haven't the faintest idea what might be in it,' said Carfax. 'Untie the knots, porter, please.'

Two or three guests hovered near, watching curiously. The hamper was unusually large, and any activities of the police aroused their interest. As the last knot was unfastened Adam, Angela and Roger appeared from upstairs and joined the little crowd. Carfax obviously wished that he had taken the hamper to a less public spot, but he threw the lid back with a flourish.

There was a moment of tense silence—and then a woman gave a cry, which she stifled quickly. Angela gripped Roger's arm. The porter said: 'It's—it's *terrible!*' Carfax stood staring into the hamper, his face chalk-white.

Inside was a woman.

Her body crouched forward, her head touching her knees, her dark hair covering her face.

Trivett said sharply: 'Clear the hall, please. Carfax, see if that van can be stopped, will you?' He glanced up, and his gaze fell on Roger. 'Macclesfield, lend me a hand, please.'

'Is she—is she *dead*?' gasped the porter.

CHAPTER 21

MESSAGE FOR DAWLISH

The woman lay in the bedroom nearest to the hall. She was not dead. Trivett had felt her pulse and made sure that it was beating. He made no comment, but Roger knew that he thought the woman had been drugged.

The van had been caught easily enough, but it belonged to a local carrier, who said that he had been told to collect the hamper from Walsham Station. The hamper had been on a London train which had left Waterloo at half-past twelve that morning. Already Trivett had been on the telephone to Scotland Yard, to trace the movements of the hamper in London. The police-surgeon diagnosed morphine poisoning administered by injection.

Before he left the photographs had arrived from Scotland Yard. The woman was Grace Hillmorton.

The second report from Scotland Yard came with the photographs. With the start which Dawlish had given them they had made surprising and disquieting discoveries. A number of wives, daughters and—in three instances—the only sons of well-known jewel-collectors had been missing from their homes for several weeks. The tally was fifteen. In four cases inquiries had already elicited the reluctant information that the jewel-collectors had recently been robbed, and that they had been blackmailed into silence by threats to their relatives. Mizzy had selected his victims cunningly; no single report had been made to the police. It was impossible to guess the total value of the stolen goods, but undoubtedly it ran into millions of pounds.

Dawlish and Felicity, Tim, Ted and Peter Boon were in the sitting-room of the cottage. The lights were on and the curtains were drawn. Tim strummed the piano lightly. Peter Boon, pale, his eyes feverishly bright, sat back in an easy-chair, his head supported by cushions, his fingers intertwining nervously.

Suddenly Dawlish said: 'Shut up, Tim.' The piano-playing stopped immediately. 'Boon, this isn't a small matter, you know—it may mean life and death to several people. It might even mean life and death to you, your brother and your sister. We're dealing with a man who has no scruples at all. Your father knew him, that's quite obvious—and it looks as if he were being blackmailed. The reason for that doesn't matter. Boon—' Dawlish leaned forward, tense and unsmiling—'you *must* tell us what you know—what your father knew—about this man Mizzy. He's always dealt through Missingham, hasn't he? And he told you and your brother enough about it to make the three of you decide to try to fight him. Right?'

Peter said: 'You're dreaming, my father didn't—'

Dawlish said: 'You're worried, aren't you? You're not talking because you're afraid of one of two things: smearing your father's memory *or* bringing suspicion on someone dear to you. Let's have the truth.'

Peter moistened his lips.

'You're crazy,' he muttered, 'there's nothing to tell. Adam had that notion about the pearls, and—'

'He had the notion for a definite reason,' said Dawlish. 'And although you fooled Macclesfield, you haven't fooled us, Boon. The decision to keep those pearls away from Carfax was made by your family. You pretended that it was Adam's idea, but it was carefully planned beforehand. The scene at the *Bay Hotel* was put on for Macclesfield's benefit. Wasn't it?'

Peter cried: 'No, no, no! Stop questioning me, I can't stand it, my head's whirling, I can't *think*.'

'You don't have to think,' said Dawlish, 'you just have to remember. And you do remember. You'll feel much better if you tell the truth.'

'I don't know anything.'

There was silence.

Dawlish stood up, a slow, deliberate movement, and stood in front of Peter with his hands in his pockets. He knew that the man was feeling ill, that he should, in fact, still be in a hospital bed. But Dawlish also knew that too much depended on making him talk to justify considering Peter Boon for his own sake.

So he said: 'All right, Boon. I'm sorry about this. I'll give you two minutes to remember, and if you haven't started to talk then I shall beat you up.'

He stood quite still. Tim, on the piano-stool, was staring at him fixedly; Ted had leaned forward, as if he were about to get up. Felicity still went on darning, but her needle was trembling, and she watched her husband from beneath her lashes. There was menace here, cold and relentless.

'Well?' said Dawlish.

Peter cried out: 'I'll tell you. God forgive me for it, I'll tell you!'

* * *

The first time he had heard of Mizzy, according to Peter Boon, was two years ago, when he and Adam had discovered that his father was being blackmailed. They had decided, at first without telling him, that they would try to find out who was at the back of it.

They had soon found 'Missingham' but they learned that it was an assumed name; he was merely an agent of the crook, not the crook himself.

But they had won something; by threatening Missingham they had eased the pressure on their father. There were no further demands for payment; but every now and again the Colonel had a telephone call warning him that he wasn't forgotten.

Angela did not know what was afoot; but the brothers thought she had some idea.

And then, out of the blue, there had come a demand; Mizzy wanted co-operation from the Boons. Adam and Peter were general merchants, they shipped goods to all parts of the world, and worked in close touch with several shipping lines. Mizzy wanted goods smuggled out of the country. And the Boons had been told that if they refused, Angela would die.

'Maybe we were crazy,' muttered Peter, 'but it would have been so easy for them to kill her, and—well, we agreed. We agreed—but we were determined to find who Mizzy was, and put an end to it. The only way was to agree to help, and wait for our chance. We took some stuff abroad, packed in big crates marked as machinery; we had to make Mizzy think that we were really playing his game. Then my father and I had an idea. Adam was in Ireland on business, so we didn't consult him. It was one of those quick ideas, and we acted right away. We took those pearls. They weren't crated like the others. They were sent to us by hand, and we were told to pack them with another consignment which was being shipped the next day.'

He paused, but no one made any comment.

'They were to go to Switzerland,' said Peter. 'We knew that Mizzy would soon learn they hadn't arrived. We didn't have any contact with the man, we only had messages by telephone, and the goods were always delivered to our warehouse unexpectedly—usually by ordinary carriers. We thought that if only we could lure Mizzy or one of his men to come after the pearls, we'd get results. Perhaps it wasn't a very sensible plan, but we were nearly off our heads with worry.'

Dawlish said: 'Yes, I can understand that.'

'We sent Angela down to Brittling to get her out of the way,' said Peter. 'Adam came back, and we told him what we'd done; he said we were crazy and we had a furious row; but it was too late then. He was afraid that Angela would be hurt, but nothing happened—absolutely *nothing* happened. That made the suspense worse.'

Dawlish said: 'Where were the pearls all this time?'

'My father kept them in his flat,' said Peter.

'What happened?' said Dawlish.

Peter went on: 'For ten days, nothing—and then we had a note from Angela, saying that she was being followed everywhere she went. You can imagine the effect on us.'

'Shattering,' murmured Dawlish.

'It shattered us all right,' agreed Peter fervently. 'We all rushed down. In fact Adam and my father came first, the night before, although they didn't tell Angela they'd arrived—they wanted to see who this man was, and stayed at another hotel, to keep watch. Nothing happened then, either. We saw Macclesfield, of course, but Adam was rather favourably impressed by him when he first saw him.'

Dawlish nodded.

'Then the Colonel was robbed,' said Peter simply. 'The

pearls were taken, but a dummy packet was left in his suitcase. It wasn't until next morning when I had arrived, and Macclesfield had had his tumble on the cliffs, that we realised the pearls were missing. And it didn't matter then, because we'd got them back. Obviously the thief had been careless and dropped them out of his pocket. You—you know what happened after that.'

'We know what happened, but we don't know why,' said Dawlish quietly.

'Why what?'

'Why you encouraged Macclesfield to get in touch with *Messrs Cumfitt, Day and Dawlish*,' said Dawlish.

Peter said quickly: 'That's easy! We'd seen the advertisement, and thought it was a trick of Mizzy's to get the pearls back. And we didn't want to respond ourselves, we weren't sure at that time whether he knew we were responsible for the pearls failing to reach Switzerland. But now that Macclesfield was there we thought we could try something. That's why we advised him to make the rendezvous with you. I was hiding with Angela just below the level of the cliff, and Adam was a few yards away. We didn't see anyone behind us, but the man who attacked us and carried Angela off must have known we were there all the time. Angela and I had crept up to the top of the cliff when he slugged me. I don't remember much after that, but the police told me what had happened. And they assured me that Angela's all right—she *is*, isn't she?'

'Quite all right. Why did you make such a fuss about telling me this?'

Peter muttered: 'Well, we have been shipping Mizzy's stuff abroad for him, and Adam—well, my father and I let Adam in for this, really. He would have talked us out of taking the pearls in the first place.'

'Ah, yes,' agreed Dawlish. 'All right, Boon—there's nothing else we want. You'd better get some sleep. As soon as we've any news, we'll pass it on.'

'Thanks,' muttered Boon.

'The question is, can we believe all he says, and if we can, where does it get us?' said Tim, swivelling round on the piano-stool and staring at Dawlish. 'I should say he told the truth, as far as he knows it, and that the Boons have been Mizzy's chief shipping agents for some time, but—how much more is there to learn from the story?' He gave the others no chance to make suggestions, but went on: 'One thing sticks out a mile—Roger Macclesfield *might* not be all he seems. Don't you agree, Ted?' He turned to the bulky man for agreement.

'I do,' said Ted, who had now slumped back in his chair. 'Watch Roger, Pat.'

Dawlish smiled, but his thoughts were obviously elsewhere.

'Oh, yes, watch him,' he said dreamily. 'But we haven't much time for watching. Much more in Peter's story than meets the eye, you know. Part of it was true. The rest . . .' He shrugged his shoulders. 'Remarkable business about the pearls, wasn't it?' He paused. 'Why *should* Mizzy, whom you'd expect to have gone right up in the air from the first, start all that business on the cliff? Car and motor-boat combined, remember. Find the answer to that, and we've found the answer to most things.'

Felicity said suddenly: 'What's that?'

She had exceptionally acute hearing, and her interruption made all of them look towards the window. There were footsteps on the drive—two people were walking towards the cottage. And as they drew nearer the four inside the room heard voices. A man's and a woman's. The couple were making no attempt to hide their approach, and Dawlish, relaxing a little, went to the door. Ted and Tim stood in the shadows behind him.

The heavy iron bell pealed through the house as Dawlish flung open the door.

There, standing on the step, stood Roger and Angela.

CHAPTER 22

TRICK OF TRIVETT'S?

'Mr Dawlish!' exclaimed Angela. 'Is that you?'

'Certainly. Come in, the pair of you.'

Dawlish stood aside, and as they entered the hall he looked along the drive, trying to peer through the gloom; but he could see no-one else behind them, and there was no light by the gates, no car, no sound of movement. He closed the door and locked it, then shot the bolts and put the chain up.

'Well,' said Dawlish. 'How did you come?'

'By bus, and then we walked from Valcoombe,' said Angela. Flushed as she was, she looked lovely, and Roger's lingering gaze was filled with admiration.

'Oh,' said Dawlish. 'You just walked out of *The George and Dragon*, caught the bus from Walsham and here you are. No salt on your tail?'

'I don't think we were followed,' said Roger quietly. 'Trivett let us come here. We've brought a message. There was a bit of a shindy between him and Carfax, because Carfax didn't want us to be allowed to come,' he added.

'Ah,' said Dawlish. 'I know Bill Trivett, and there isn't a better cop in England. He wouldn't row with a provincial copper in front of you or anyone else unless he had some murky purpose in mind. However, we'll come to that later—what made him give you his blessing?'

Angela said: 'She's free.'

'Very helpful,' Dawlish said drily. 'She's free, but who is she?'

'Grace Hillmorton!' cried Angela.

'Grace—' began Dawlish.

Felicity appeared from the drawing-room, with Ted behind her.

Angela said quickly: 'She's all right. I mean, she's ill, she'd been drugged with morphine, but she isn't dead and she isn't seriously hurt.'

'Well, well, well!' murmured Dawlish. 'This is too much—much, much, too much. Let's go into the other room and sit and drink and think,' he went on, 'and while we're doing it Angela or Roger can tell us the story.'

He led the way into the sitting-room.

Angela began to talk.

Ted brought in the glasses, and solemnly poured out. No one interrupted Angela. When the story was finished, Ted handed Dawlish a glass of beer, and the big man put it to his lips and tossed it down.

'Well, well,' he said again.

Roger looked from one to the other.

'Well, what's the matter? You wanted the woman to be set free, didn't you?'

'Yes, of course,' said Dawlish, 'but not quite in this way. It doesn't add up. She should have been returned to me, and then I would have let Gale go. It appears to me that there's some nasty work going on, and I haven't yet cottoned on to it. Let's try to get down to the basic facts. Trivett released you. He didn't, ostensibly, follow you. He put up a pretence of rowing with Carfax so that you should think his decision sprang either out of the goodness of his heart, or because he wanted me to know about Grace. But he didn't do it for that reason, you know. He could easily have let us know without sending you. No, my children, you have been trailed here, and the police know—or soon will know—where the cottage is.'

'But we *weren't* followed,' protested Angela.

'You didn't notice that you were followed,' corrected Dawlish. 'But what I can't fathom is why Bill Trivett elected to do it this way. And why Grace was sent to Carfax.' He pondered a moment. 'Mizzy would hardly expect me to honour the bond after he'd sent Grace to Carfax. That means that he doesn't give a rap what happens to Gale. Reasonable enough, so far, isn't it?' he asked, and looked round the company as if for approval.

'I'll go so far with you,' said Ted. 'More beer?'

'Thanks.' Dawlish handed over his empty glass. 'Now listen to a little bit more. Mizzy no longer cares what happens to Gale, and has sent Grace Hillmorton back. Therefore, he had no further use for Grace. Therefore, he's disposed of the Hillmorton jewels—except, of course, the pearls. Anyone prepared to argue about that?'

Roger said quickly: 'Of course not, you're almost certainly right!'

'Generous of you,' murmured Dawlish, 'and I rather agree with you, Roger! And that suggests that Mizzy knows the game is up, and is on his way out. He's still got plenty of hostages to use as barter for his own safety; God help those people if he has any serious trouble, unless we can get at him right away. But—' he smiled—'I think we can get him right away.'

Tim said caustically: 'As easy as that?'

'I know Mizzy,' said Dawlish simply.

Angela cried: 'You know—' Her voice trailed off.

'Just another guess, darling?' said Felicity.

'If you like,' said Dawlish. 'I think the best thing to do is to take Trivett into our confidence.' He stretched out for the telephone. 'It's got to be now or never, and Mizzy doesn't know that *we—know—Mizzy*!' He frowned slightly—and then the frown turned into a scowl, as he took the receiver from his ear.

'Dead,' he announced. He looked meaningly at Tim and Ted. 'Doors, boys. Roger, you're sure you didn't see anyone on your heels when you came along?'

'Quite sure,' said Roger. This news sent alarm searing through him, and the astonishing change in the atmosphere made it even worse. 'Do you mean the line's been cut?'

'Cut or otherwise put out of order,' said Dawlish, 'and I don't think the police would have done it.'

The curtains billowed inward at the sudden opening of the door. Missingham bustled into the room.

'My *dear* Major Dawlish, how are you?' He waved a plump hand. 'I have that honour—that very great honour—of meeting you once again. Although probably Gale will shortly assume responsibility. He has just been released—one gets so stiff after being tied up for so long, doesn't one? So, Major Dawlish, you think you know who Mizzy is?'

'You have good hearing,' said Dawlish. 'How did you get in?'

'As a matter of fact,' said Missingham confidingly, 'it was rather difficult, because you have wired up the windows very well, but among Mizzy's henchmen are some of the best— the *very* best—cracksmen in England. In short, we came in through a window. We have been here since darkness fell, watching—and I may say we were delighted when we saw dear Angela and poor Macclesfield arrive. And I'm told—I do hope it's true—that you have Mr Peter Boon here, also.'

'Peter!' cried Angela. 'Where—'

'Peter's all right,' Dawlish said reassuringly.

'You're all safe enough, for the time being,' said Missingham with a bland smile. 'I *do* hope none of your friends will be foolish enough to use violence, Major Dawlish. As you will see, you are outnumbered three to one this time, and we have taken no chances—no chances at all. We are also armed.' He patted his pocket. 'Well, here we are, all bursting to hear you name Mizzy.'

Dawlish said: 'I can name Mizzy all right.'

'*Do* try!' urged Missingham. 'You were saying that Mizzy is—'

Dawlish said heavily: 'Lord Hillmorton.'

'Well, well, well!' exclaimed Missingham, a slow smile curving his lips. 'What a romantic guess! A member of the peerage. And *why* should you think that so eminent a member of the gilded chamber should be the—ah—notorious Mizzy? Do explain.'

Dawlish said: 'He let his daughter go free. He told me that rigmarole about being robbed because he knew that I was already interested in him—I started to work for Mayfair; you didn't know that, did you? I'm really looking for Penny Mayfair, and I pretended to believe Hillmorton because it seemed wise to string him along.'

'Indeed!' oozed Missingham. 'Very ingenious. I am sure his lordship will be most flattered when he discovers what you think about him. But then, perhaps he'll never know. You see, Dawlish, I don't believe you. I don't think you have ever suspected Lord Hillmorton. I am just a little afraid that you *might* be near the truth, and so this visit was planned to make sure that you can never pass it on.'

Felicity walked quietly across the room to Dawlish's side.

'Of course, of course, you may both die together,' said Missingham. 'I would never let it be said that Mizzy parted man and wife—oh dear, no! Yes, you can die together, all of you. And two of the Boons and Roger Macclesfield, all of whom *might* know too much. What a pity Adam Boon isn't here! However, we will get him eventually. Dawlish, would you like to know what we propose to do?'

'I see you are longing to tell me,' said Dawlish. 'I would never let it be said that I disappointed you.'

'Very wise, my dear Dawlish, very wise. Well, you were right up to a point. Mizzy has amassed a considerable fortune, and will retire—that's the word, retire.' Missingham seemed delighted with it. 'He will keep those hostages for a little while, in case the police *should* discover something, although I think that most unlikely. And, Dawlish, the *only* people who know he has worked, and what he has done, are the Boon family and Macclesfield—quite accidentally, poor fellow—and you and your friends. Most of you being here altogether, we can make a quick, neat job of your despatch. And you yourself put the idea into our heads—the method, that is.'

Dawlish said nothing.

Missingham went on: 'This time it won't be a bluff, and you won't be able to escape. This house, as I think has already been noticed, is old and dry. It will burn very quickly. And we shall round off the whole thing by leaving a confession from Peter Boon and his sister that they, sometimes together, sometimes singly, are really—Mizzy!'

Angela cried: 'You can't do that! You can't—'

'Oh, but we can,' said Missingham. 'I shall get Peter to sign it soon; he will gladly do that because I shall tell him that it is the only way in which he can save his sister's life. Very loyal, these Boons, aren't they? A charming family! And it will be assumed, Major Dawlish, that there was a struggle here, and a fire was started accidentally.'

A shot broke across his words, loud and sharp. It came from outside, and, momentarily distracted, Missingham's glance shifted. As it did so Dawlish lunged forward and caught him by the shoulders. Hugging the man's body to him as a shield he backed towards a corner.

'Get behind me, Fel! Get behind me!'

Tim, at the window, snatched aside the curtains and fired. The report of his shot, the crack and tinkle of breaking glass and a man's shout, smashed the quiet. In the hall something thudded heavily; a man screamed; a third shot rang out.

Then Ted Beresford staggered into the room, his cheek dripping blood. Two gunmen followed him.

CHAPTER 23

ROGER

The picture in front of Roger's eyes was like a scene in a film. Every detail stood out. Dawlish, with his wife close behind him, holding the helpless Missingham in front of him. Tim at the parted curtain. Ted Beresford, who had pitched forward and lay on the floor. Two gunmen by the door, obviously baffled by the turn of events. And Angela, close to his side.

The first of the two gunmen said shrilly:

'Let Missingham go!' He glared at Dawlish.

The other gunman took a step nearer Roger and Angela, covering them.

The curtains shifted and a man's leg appeared, through the window. The next moment a third gunman clambered in. Tim backed away, so that he protected Dawlish on one side.

The man from the window said: 'If you don't let him go—'

'One doesn't throw away a shield and a weapon,' said Dawlish in a surprisingly mild voice.

Angela looked anxiously at Roger.

'Don't—don't do anything,' she muttered.

'Whassat?' One of the gunmen swung round. 'A croak

out of any of you and I'll pump you full of lead.' Silly, melo-dramatic words—but he meant them. His little bright eyes were venomous, and Roger realised that he was so baffled by Missingham's plight that he might shoot them, just for the sake of venting his spleen.

The gunman's eyes flickered to the door, and Roger, following their gaze, saw Gale half-staggering into the room. He was carrying a half-empty tankard of beer and suddenly, furiously, he flung it at Dawlish.

'Let him go!' he yelled, half-derisively. 'It won't help you to hold out. How much do you think Missingham matters? Not that much!' He snapped his fingers, and everyone in the room except Missingham himself—and Ted—heard what he said. All looked at the hapless man who had once called himself the great Mizzy. The purple tinge had spread from his lips to his chin and his cheeks, his eyes were bulging.

Dawlish moved his stranglehold from Missingham's neck, but his grip on him was as strong. He seized the plump man's right arm and twisted it behind him, holding his victim in a half-Nelson.

'If you haven't put him down in three minutes, Dawlish, I'll shoot you through him. That'll be hard on Missingham, but it won't help you.'

Did he mean it? wondered Roger.

Of course he meant it!

There had been that shot in the grounds.

Why?

Because Mizzy's men knew that someone else was in the grounds. *Had* the police followed them? If one policeman had managed to get to Valcoombe and then walked towards the cottage, it might prove their salvation. Of course, Dawlish was hoping that would happen. *One* policeman might have ventured near enough to the cottage to find out what was happening, and then made off towards the village to summon help. In such an emergency he wouldn't waste time in telephoning Walsham or Brittling; he would round up the able-bodied men of the village—if he had any sense. Dawlish had seized on that slender hope, believing that time was all-important.

Gale said coldly: 'One minute to go, Dawlish.'

Yes, he meant it.

Dawlish would have to drop Missingham now, and once that happened he would be helpless, all of them would be in Gale's power. Roger took his arm from Angela's waist, very slowly, anxious that it shouldn't be noticed. Only one thing to do now. Before the man ordered the shooting he must jump forward. He could reach Gale and the gunman in a single leap. And if he started things, then Dawlish and Tim wouldn't be long in backing him up.

Everyone's attention was focussed on waiting for that fateful, final command. It gave Roger the chance he wanted. He jumped forward.

Crack!

A bullet smacked into the wall where Roger had been standing. Angela dropped to her knees. Roger struck out and caught Gale a stinging blow on the side of the face. Gale pitched forward. Dawlish let out a tremendous bellow. He picked Missingham up bodily and flung him towards the three men who had rushed into the room at the sound of alarm. One fell, making the others tumble over him. The gunman who had been covering Roger had his revolver only a few inches from Roger's head, his finger on the trigger—and Tim fired. The man gasped and fell back. Next moment the room was in an uproar.

It looked as if that hundredth chance was coming off—but

a new sound barked above the din of the struggle, an ominous note which made everyone—even Dawlish—pause.

Rat-tat-tat-tat-tat.

Machine-gun!

A man stood outside the window, with the gun in his arms.

Gale hadn't been badly hurt. Of the gunmen, only one appeared to be in serious pain, and his right arm hung by his side. Missingham lay on the floor without moving—and Beresford hadn't stirred throughout the *mélée*. Gale stood by the door directing his men. Beresford and Missingham were dragged into a corner out of the way. Dawlish, Tim and Roger were tied to chairs. The cords bit into Roger's flesh and he couldn't move.

'What about the women?' asked one of the men.

'We'll take them with us,' said Gale. He laughed. 'Hear that, Dawlish? We're taking your wife with us. Maybe she'll appeal to Mizzy, maybe she won't. And *maybe* she would appeal to me—but there's plenty of time to worry about that. Ever heard of a spot called Buenos Aires? Where all the bad girls go?' He laughed again. He was flushed and his eyes glittered; he was at the peak of his triumph, almost drunk with it. 'Bad show for you, Dawlish; this time you've bitten off more than you can chew.'

Dawlish said: 'I wouldn't be too sure, Gale.'

'I'm dead sure,' sneered Gale. He looked at one of his men. 'Go and get Boon,' he ordered, and then glanced at the man with the tommy-gun. 'What happened outside?' he demanded. 'What was the shooting about?'

'We had a couple of visitors,' said the man. 'Want 'em here?'

'Yes,' said Gale.

He didn't ask who they were.

The police, thought Roger hopelessly. The police had come

after him and Angela, but the grounds had been too well watched for them to get away for help. Surely it couldn't end like this! Dawlish, Beresford, Tim, the two newcomers, Peter Boon and he—murdered. And Angela? His flesh crept, it was unbearable—worse because Angela and Felicity stood side by side, looking composed, serene—lovely. They weren't of the same world as Gale and his men.

The front door opened, there were footsteps, and then the room door opened. Cedric Forbes was thrust unceremoniously forward, and after him came Adam Boon.

CHAPTER 24

ADAM

'Adam!' cried Angela, then caught her breath.

Adam glanced at her; there was the faintest hint of a smile on his lips, but it soon disappeared. He had obviously been struggling with his captors—and so had Forbes. Adam's collar and tie were halfway round his neck, and his coat was torn. He looked at Gale.

'Will someone tell me what all this is about?'

'Just a little party we're preparing,' said Gale. 'We wanted you to come along and complete it—we aren't sorry to see Forbes, either.'

Adam stepped to Angela's side and took her hands.

'And it's my fault,' he said in a low-pitched voice. 'It's all my fault.'

'Oh, Adam!'

'If you've finished crying on each other's shoulder, you can break up,' rasped Gale. He nodded to one of his men, who strode across and dragged Adam away. He made no attempt to struggle, but faced Gale.

'Don't hurt her,' he said.

'Oh, I wouldn't hurt a hair of her head,' said Gale, 'she's much too precious!' He laughed hoarsely. 'I'll fix him, you fix Forbes,' he added to his men. He set to work on securing Adam. 'How did you get here?' he demanded.

Adam said: 'You'd like to know, wouldn't you?'

'O.K. If that's how you want it.' Gale stretched out towards Angela, and seized a handful of her hair. Angela gasped with pain. Gale tugged at it again, then turned and faced Adam.

'How did you get here?' he demanded.

Adam said: 'All right, Gale, but you'll suffer for that. Forbes brought me. There was some brooha going on among the police, and I slipped away. Forbes was standing in the doorway of a tea-shop—'

'Tea-shop?'

'As I have said, a tea-shop,' repeated Adam. 'He told me that he knew where Dawlish was—I wanted to see Dawlish and he wanted to get away. So I hired a car and we came as far as Valcoombe, then walked.' He glanced at Forbes's bandaged ankle, but said nothing more.

'Were you followed?' demanded Gale.

'No.'

'Where's that dame?'

'Dame?' echoed Adam, as if mystified.

'The woman who came to see you, who's staying at the pub,' said Gale. 'Come on, let's have it—where is she?'

'Still there, I hope,' said Adam.

He spoke stiffly, glanced again at Angela, then snapped: 'Get on with what you're doing!'

Gale said: 'In our own good time. We're waiting for Mizzy.'

He broke off at the sound of a car changing gear. Tension rose again; the imminence of personal disaster seemed to recede. Even Mizzy's men were affected. Roger observed all this without thinking very clearly. He knew that it was no use hoping for rescue; he was convinced that Gale and his men would win. And the end would come soon, at this cottage. He felt a wild desire to laugh. If only he had told the police just where the cottage was!

Gale said importantly: 'That'll be Mizzy. Get ready for a shock, Dawlish. Like to know something? *I've* never seen Mizzy, either. Going to be a red-letter day for me too.'

The car drew nearer.

Gale said: 'One of you, open the door.'

The car tyres scraped on the gravel. A door slammed. Someone walked lightly across the porch and into the hall. A man exclaimed, as if in surprise, but the newcomer didn't speak. Everyone eyed the door; Adam with mounting tension, Roger with a terrible feeling of hopelessness.

Ruth Marraday came in.

She was as cool and composed as when Roger had first seen her, and Adam had welcomed her with such delight. She stood, now, in the middle of the room, stripping off her gloves.

Gale said hoarsely: '*You're* Mizzy!'

Ruth smiled.

'No, just a messenger,' she said, 'he'll be here.' She looked round her. 'So you've got them all, Gale—that's good. Dawlish, too—you've given us quite a run, Dawlish, there were times when we were really worried.' She turned sharply to Gale. 'Why aren't the women tied up?'

'Ruth!' cried Angela.

Ruth Marraday ignored her.

Gale said thickly: 'I didn't think Mizzy—'

'You were told to get them *all*,' said Ruth. 'Didn't you receive the message?'

'Yes, but—'

'It isn't your job to think,' said Ruth. 'That is done for you. You know we're going to set fire to the cottage?'

'Yes—yes, that's right,' said Gale.

'Then get the things ready,' said Ruth.

Gale strode to the door and gave orders to the men outside. As he was doing so Ruth looked dispassionately at Missingham, and when Gale came back she asked:

'What happened to him?'

'Dawlish got rough.'

Ruth shrugged.

'Well, Missingham doesn't matter much, his usefulness is over in any case.' The callousness of the woman made Roger writhe. 'Well, Dawlish, you were the first one to discover that we were blackmailing the victims into silence, weren't you? Now I've some news for you. We've sold everything we've taken in the last two years—*everything*. We're ready to leave. I won't tell you where we're going, but we'll be a long way from England, and the English police won't be able to touch us. We've piled up a fortune abroad. But before we go we'll make a clean sweep.'

'Maybe,' said Dawlish.

Ruth Marraday flashed: 'There's no "maybe" about it! This is the end of your meteoric career.'

Men came in scattering piles of loose straw which they arranged in four huge bonfires. No one spoke while this was being done. An air of absolute finality rested upon the room. Roger couldn't believe what he saw, and yet he knew, coldly and reasoningly, that Mizzy's mob meant to destroy everyone who had opposed them.

And now Peter Boon was brought into the room.

'Ruth—'

Ruth said: 'Never mind the talk, Peter. Tie him up,' she ordered Gale.

'Ruth! What on earth—' Peter broke off, his eyes aflame with horror. 'Ruth, you can't be serious. You can't do a thing like this to us. To Adam, to Angela—you—you can't! We've never done anything to you, we've always—'

'Be quiet,' said Ruth impatiently.

Men seized Peter, but he began to struggle.

'We always did what Mizzy told us,' he cried, 'we only went wrong once. You can't do this, the pearls aren't worth anything compared with the rest, you can't do it! Ruth!' He tried to get up, but his bonds were too tight. 'Ruth, you can't do this to us. To Adam—'

'Light the fires,' Ruth ordered.

Gale said: 'But Mizzy—'

'Light the fires! If he's coming, okay; if he isn't, it doesn't matter, I know what he wants. Light the fires.'

Gale took a box of matches from his pocket, but hesitated as if now that they had really come to the moment he could not bring himself to start the flames. Ruth snatched the matches from him, struck one, and carried it to the nearest heap of straw. But as she bent down it went out.

'Ruth, I'll do anything—anything!' cried Peter. 'Don't let me die like this. I'll go on helping Mizzy—won't we, Adam? Won't we?'

Adam said harshly: 'We'll work for him all right.'

'You see, Adam agrees,' gasped Peter.

She struck another match.

'*Ruth!*' screamed Peter.

Someone in the hall began to cough.

Peter went on screaming. Adam, absolutely calm now, watched him coldly. Angela turned her head away. The match flared up, and Ruth carried it nearer to the pile of tinder-dry stuff. The man outside began to cough more violently.

'What's happening out there?' called Gale loudly.

'Dunno,' a man answered. 'I—'

He broke off, and was taken by a fit of coughing. Ruth dropped the match on to the pile. The straw caught and flames began to lick savagely.

Dawlish looked up into his wife's face and *winked*.

CHAPTER 25

MIZZY

Dawlish knew why they were coughing.

Dawlish had planned . . .

Gale turned back into the room, clutching at his throat, tears streaming down his face. A whitish vapour spread over the room, curling from the doorway.

The fire blazed up, crackling fiercely.

With one deft movement Adam freed himself.

Doubled up with coughing, nobody in the room saw him. Only the man at the window, still untouched by the gas, was unaffected. He raised his gun—and Adam snapped at him:

'Get away while you can, you fool.'

He bent down, snatched a carpet from the floor and flung it over the burning pile. Smoke as well as the gas filled the room now.

And then a figure appeared in the doorway—grotesque in a gas-mask. And there were others, two of whom carried guns.

They cut Dawlish's bonds and flung the windows wide.

A draught of clear air blew across the room. Tear-gas, Roger thought vaguely, they had released tear-gas. There was no danger now, just a bad half-hour and then it would be all over, but—how had these men entered?

Dawlish had planned all this . . .

'They were here all the time,' said Dawlish. 'Upstairs in the loft. I was pretty sure that Mizzy's mob would come again, and had this little bag of tricks fixed up. It seemed the only way to get Mizzy,' he added. 'And it did.'

The significance of that 'and it did' failed to impress Roger at first. The room was clear of smoke and tear-gas, the fire was out. The gunmen were locked up in the garage.

He said weakly: 'Who *are* they?'

'Just friends,' said Dawlish. 'Always glad to help out when we get into a spot. We stayed at the cottage to draw Mizzy. If everyone else had been caught and Mizzy remained free, it wouldn't have helped much. Because I've no doubt your friend Ruth—'

'*Friend*,' gasped Adam. 'Draw it mild.'

Dawlish said: 'All right, just Ruth! She told the truth about being ready with Mizzy to leave the country, and undoubtedly they've a fortune salted away in South America. We—'

'Sat here like spiders drawing the flies,' said Forbes. 'But don't run it quite so close again, Pat. Nearest I've ever been to Kingdom Come. Did I hear you say that you *had* unmasked Mizzy?'

'Yes.'

'Then who—'

'It's Ruth, of course,' said Adam. 'Didn't Gale say that he always had his orders from a woman?'

Dawlish said: 'You do get women like that sometimes. Probably a psychopathic case.' He laughed, without humour. 'I've never seen a more cold-blooded piece in my life, I'll hand that to her.'

The woman did not speak.

She sat in an easy-chair, her hair tumbled, her face smeared by smoke.

'And I—I was in love with her,' muttered Adam. He walked towards her, and there was silence in the room. 'Ruth, why did you do it? You would have killed Angela—Peter—*me*. I can't understand it.' He stretched out his hand.

Dawlish flashed across the room, and pulled his hand away. Adam swung round angrily.

'I think you can understand plenty,' said Dawlish in a mild voice. 'Don't you think he does, Ruth?' The woman looked up at him sullenly, without speaking. 'Yes, you can understand plenty, Adam Boon. After all, you should do. You're Mizzy.'

Adam snapped: 'I've never heard anything so preposterous—'

'Oh, but you *are* Mizzy,' said Dawlish patiently. 'Like to see the proof?'

Adam reared up, his eyes blazing. But he had lost too much time. Dawlish grabbed his wrist, snatched his hand out of his pocket—and a gun clattered to the floor.

No one spoke.

Adam's harsh breathing was the only sound.

Ruth leaned forward in her chair, staring up at him.

Angela stood quite still.

Roger thought: It can't be true, it can't be true!

Dawlish stretched out his right hand and took a dry leaf from the side of Adam's beard.

'To be betrayed by such a tiny thing,' he said quietly. 'Yes, Boon, when you met Angela and Roger at *The George and Dragon* you had a creeper leaf sticking on your beard. One of my friends saw it. They always mention odd little things like that—and this one told us the truth. *You killed your father.* You made it look like suicide. You locked the door and bolted it, took the pearls and climbed from his window to that of your own room. The only trace you showed was the creeper leaf; that particular variety grows only on that particular wall of *The George and Dragon*. Little things mean so much, don't they?'

Adam said: 'It's a lie!'

Dawlish shrugged.

'There are other things. It was your idea to send for *Cumfitt, Day and Dawlish* because, as Mizzy, you suspected I had put in the advertisement and you were anxious to find out what I knew. Then you went with Peter and Angela to the meeting place. Remarkable thing—you were supposed to be keeping your eyes open in case of trouble, but you let Peter be hurt, let a man carry off Angela—you *allowed* it, Boon.'

Adam said: 'You're crazy!' But his voice lacked confidence now.

Dawlish went on: 'And then you had that quarrel with Roger. Roger virtually accused you of being responsible; for a moment you thought he'd guessed the truth—and you couldn't keep your temper. Then you realised he wasn't thinking of that, he'd no idea—so he wasn't a danger after all, and you made it up. Want more? Well, there's Ruth, of course—so deeply in love with you that she would have let herself be damned as Mizzy. But you have a spark of affection for her, and you just dropped a tablet into her lap.' He opened his hand, and a tiny white pellet lay on his palm. 'What is it? Cyanide? Something that would have killed her right off, anyhow—and she would be Mizzy, a dead Mizzy. And you would be as free as the air.'

Ruth closed her eyes.

'And Gale knew you were in the racket,' Dawlish said. 'He tied you up—but you weren't really secure, he didn't make good knots for you.'

'Any more?' asked Forbes lightly.

'Some odds and ends,' said Dawlish still talking to Adam. 'Chiefly about the pearls. Your father and Peter, who had no idea of the truth at the time, thought they were smart about the pearls. But when you discovered it there was a hell of a row— Peter told us that tonight. So I should think you had a special customer waiting for those pearls. But you were troubled by the advertisement in *The Times* by then. You wondered whether it was a police trick or whether I was behind it. You thought it would be a bright idea if you answered it. It was worth losing the pearls to get a line on *Cumfitt, Day and Dawlish*, and you felt sure you could persuade Roger to answer the advertisement. Roger was a gift from the gods—a go-between whom the police might suspect, and with whom I might deal while you watched. You hoped to find out how much I knew through Roger and those pearls. And you felt that, whatever the risk, you had to find that out. And as Roger had shown such interest in Angela he was the right Aunt Sally. However, I told him only as much as I wanted him to tell you. That I might use the cottage again, for instance. You were so anxious to finish me off, and were bound to raid me here. Oh, you wanted Roger to get those pearls. You fixed the whole business; they weren't dropped by accident, they were planted on the cliff. You knew of Roger's interest in Angela. You instructed Gale to wait for the best chance to get them together—and the chance came very quickly, that very morning. It was easy to hire a motor-boat, just to confuse the police. In fact, Gale went back by car. All true, isn't it, Boon?'

Adam did not answer.

'And this final thing,' said Dawlish in a very hard voice. 'Your father discovered the truth about you. I think he had suspected it for some time. That was why he took the pearls and left the hotel without a word to Roger. He didn't want Roger mixed up in it any further. At last you discovered that he could name you as Mizzy, so you killed him. And I think he was glad to die, because of the shame,' said Dawlish gently. 'Because—'

Adam growled: 'You seem to know everything, but you're just guessing.'

'He told someone he suspected you,' said Dawlish. 'He told *me*. I advertised for the pearls because he told me about them. Lord Hillmorton confirmed that his daughter was wearing them when she disappeared, that's all. Boon, no one could have sunk lower than you. You started this whole business by blackmailing your own father.'

Angela gave a low cry, full of pain.

'Your father was, at one time, a receiver of stolen goods,' went on Dawlish relentlessly. 'He'd lived it down. Adam discovered it. Only one of the family could have done that. Later on—at *The George and Dragon*—only you, Roger or Angela could have let Mizzy know about my bargain with Gale. I was sure of Roger and pretty sure of Angela—and then I heard about the leaf in your beard.' He paused, and then asked: 'Where are the other women prisoners, Boon?'

Adam said: 'So you've got to that.' He shook himself free from Tim's restraining hand. 'I wondered when you'd realise your case wasn't so strong, Dawlish. You've always worked independently of the police against me, and you can go on doing it—because if you tell the police, if you stop me from getting away, you'll never see any of those women again.' He laughed. 'Understand, Dawlish? My life against theirs—there are fourteen persons altogether, hidden quite safely.'

'Adam—' began Angela. But she couldn't go on, and Adam took no notice of her.

'I've sent them somewhere *quite* safe,' he repeated. 'None of my men knows where they are, I've taken every precaution.

Well, what's it to be?' When Dawlish didn't answer, Adam burst into gusty laughter, but his eyes were glinting; he wasn't sane, he *couldn't* be sane. 'Well, what's it to be?' he repeated. 'You're so full of the milk of human kindness, aren't you? Fourteen people—eleven women and three boys—and only I can release them. If they're not released they won't live long. *Now* who holds the aces, Dawlish?'

Then Ruth opened her eyes.

'They're at a house in Berkshire,' she began, 'called—'

'Ruth! Don't tell them!' Adam swung round on her. 'It's our only chance.'

'*Highways*, on the Oxford side of Reading,' said Ruth in a flat voice.

About an hour after that final scene in the cottage, the telephone-bell rang in Trivett's room at *The George and Dragon*. He was sitting by the side of his bed, glancing through the latest report which stated that Roger and Angela had left the bus at Valcoombe, and were at a place called Valley Cottage. The police were gathering to raid the cottage, but Trivett was worried. Would they find Dawlish? Could Dawlish escape the consequences of his high-handed behaviour? If Mizzy were caught through his activities—yes. If not—no. Trivett wasn't at all happy. But he'd given the big man as much rope as he dared.

'Trivett speaking,' he said into the telephone.

'Hallo, Bill,' said the voice of Patrick Dawlish. 'Haven't disturbed your beauty sleep, I hope.'

'Oh, it's you, is it?' answered Trivett heavily. 'And what piece of madness are you up to now?'

'I've a present for you. If you go to Valley Cottage, near Valcoombe, you'll find Mizzy and his merry men all tied up, with a woman named Ruth Marraday, who's been staying at *The*

George and Dragon under your very eyes. Go easy with her, Bill. I don't think she knew a thing about Boon's murder.'

'Thanks,' said Trivett drily. 'And you expect me to believe that you've got Mizzy?'

'*I* haven't got him—he's waiting at the cottage for the police to come and collect him,' Dawlish said mildly.

Trivett said: 'Pat, I'm not sure that you haven't gone too far this time. Carfax is raging mad. He'll probably win the ear of his Chief Constable.'

'And you'll get a stiff reprimand,' said Dawlish apologetically. 'Sorry, Bill, but it had to be done. Thanks for your patience. If the local cops get awkward I'll have to fight it out, but if you make sure of Mizzy and his mob, that'll serve me in good stead. Keep me out of the dock if you can, though. Oh—Roger Macclesfield and Angela Boon should be back at *The George and Dragon* soon. I'm delivering Peter Boon back to hospital, he's not feeling too good. With him goes Ted Beresford, hurt rather badly, but he'll pull through.'

'Ted's there on his own responsibility,' said Trivett, 'but you were crazy to move Peter Boon. If he should take a turn for the worse—'

'*Will* you worry about what has to be done, not what might happen?' implored Dawlish.

'I'll see what I can do,' said Trivett. 'Now, what *is* all this about Mizzy? You're not serious?' But he was smiling.

'My dear chap! The man with the creeper leaf in his beard. Observe the small things—and remind Carfax that if he'd noticed that he might have made the arrest himself. Adam Boon, no other. Oh, yes, full confession—and a statement from his lady, which would in itself be enough to damn him. And— but I nearly forgot! All the missing odds and ends are at a house called *Highways*, on the Oxford side of Reading. Adam worked from there. He spent a lot of time travelling, ostensibly for his business, actually on his crookery. Strange man. But I must fly, Bill—Felicity's calling.'

'Darling,' said Angela, 'you mustn't be absurd. It's nearly six months ago, and everything's cleared up. Peter needs a partner in the business, and, in spite of what's happened, it is an honest business and if anyone's earned a share it's you.'

It was a fine, crisp day, late in March. They stood on the edge of the cliff, as they had done six months before.

Angela squared her shoulders.

'And as I was saying, darling, Peter needs a partner, he'll never have the strength to carry on the business alone.'

Roger laughed, and kissed her.

'Then you'll join him?' asked Angela eagerly.

'Yes, of course. I'd be a mug if I didn't,' said Roger. 'But before we sign on the dotted line, darling, are you sure—really *sure*—that you want to marry me? Six months ago you were excited and keyed up, and I've a miserable fear that since then you've just decided you can't go back on your word.'

Angela hugged him.

'I'm so very sure,' she said.

ABOUT THE AUTHOR

John Creasey, born in 1908, was a paramount English crime and science fiction writer who used myriad pseudonyms for more than six hundred novels. He founded the UK Crime Writers' Association in 1953. In 1962, his book *Gideon's Fire* received the Edgar Award for Best Novel from the Mystery Writers of America. Many of the characters featured in Creasey's titles became popular, including George Gideon of Scotland Yard, who was the basis for a subsequent television series and film. Creasey died in Salisbury, UK, in 1973.

THE PATRICK DAWLISH MYSTERIES

FROM OPEN ROAD MEDIA

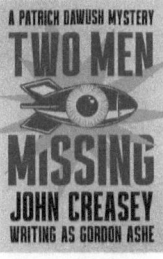  

INTEGRATED MEDIA

Find a full list of our authors and
titles at www.openroadmedia.com

FOLLOW US
@OpenRoadMedia